LOVERS IN THE AGE
OF INDIFFERENCE

Xiaolu Guo

Chatto & Windus
LONDON

Published by Chatto & Windus 2010

2 4 6 8 10 9 7 5 3 1

A version of the story 'An Internet Baby' was printed in
*Freedom: Short Stories Celebrating the Universal Declaration of
Human Rights*, published by Amnesty, 2009.

First published in Great Britain in 2010 by
Chatto & Windus
Random House, 20 Vauxhall Bridge Road,
London SW1V 2SA

www.rbooks.co.uk

Addresses for companies within The Random House
Group Limited can be found at:
www.randomhouse.co.uk/offices.htm

The Random House Group Limited Reg. No. 954009

A CIP catalogue record for this book
is available from the British Library

ISBN 9780701184834

The Random House Group Limited makes every effort to
ensure that the papers used in its books are made from trees that
have been legally sourced from well-managed and credibly
certified forests. Our paper procurement policy can be found at:
www.rbooks.co.uk/environment

Mixed Sources
Product group from well-managed
forests and other controlled sources
www.fsc.org Cert no. TT-COC-2139
© 1996 Forest Stewardship Council

Printed in Great Britain by
Clays Ltd, St Ives plc

CONTENTS

For the last ten years, on the journey from east to west, from country to country, these stories have embedded themselves in my body.

THE MOUNTAIN KEEPER

The Mountain Keeper is nameless. People just call him the man who watches over the mountain.

He might have come from Cangzhou in Hebei Province, or maybe from Anyang in Henan Province. He could be from any corner of China that manufactures migrant workers. He is tanned but slightly emaciated. He is young but his expression is tinged with indifference and apathy.

He has been more fortunate than his fellow villagers. They have come to Beijing to build highways or lay concrete on the 5th Ring Road. Burnt and boiled by the blazing sun, they dig holes and haul rocks. And he is perched high in the clouds under the shade of leafy trees. The city dust and the construction noise are like his home town – too far away to touch. He is the Mountain Keeper.

Every day he sits on the summit of Red Snail Mountain.

Surrounding him are trees, nothing but trees. Every morning he ascends the tranquil and lonesome mountain and gazes down at the Beijing suburbs below. He is perched so high, as high as an eagle, with Huairou County lying stretched out beneath him, the colour of sand, the smell of cement. He surveys the lands below; watching everything but seeing nothing.

The Mountain Keeper wonders at his mountain's name: Red Snail Mountain. Why is it called that? There are no red snails up there, he thinks, there aren't even any black snails. Snails live in gardens or rivers or streams, don't they? Or do they hide away in rocky crevices? Maybe the mountain is home to the spirits of the red snails. Spirits that haunt the Red Snail Temple nestled on the mountainside. Enclosed by broad walls and sheltered by wild bamboo groves. It's an empty, desolate place. There are never even any monks around.

Once upon a time Red Snail Temple was a place of legend. The Mountain Keeper talks to himself about it sometimes. Looking down through the blanket of smog smothering the ground below, he sees the green paddy fields covered in soil. He can hear the sounds of distant car horns but he remains lonesome. He was told in his training that Red Snail Temple was built during the Eastern Jin Dynasty. The Eastern Jin was more than 1,500 years ago; the Mountain Keeper can't start to imagine what things were like back then. Did the rich journey in sedan chairs? Did servants fan their masters with swan feathers? Did imperial officials wear peaked caps and high

2

boots? The Mountain Keeper loses his thoughts in the ethereal clouds.

During the Mountain Keeper's training the Park Ranger had told him with a grave face that the history of the mountain was hugely significant. If he wanted to work there he would have to memorise key facts so that he could pass his knowledge on to visitors. The Park Ranger then started to read from his book of mountain data: '"Red Snail Temple was built during the Eastern Jin Dynasty in AD 348." You must remember to mention Eastern Jin, otherwise sightseers will come and ask you and you will look like an illiterate.'

Eastern Jin is Eastern Jin, the young Mountain Keeper thought, what's so hard to remember about that? He never really saw what Eastern Jin had to do with his mountain, but every day he walked past the temple's peeling walls and whispered daringly: Is it really over a thousand years old? Is it really home to ghosts and spirits?

When the Mountain Keeper was little he'd learnt an old poem from his school textbook:

> No matter how deep the water
> As long as a dragon dwells in it.
> No matter how high the mountain
> As long as a spirit rests on it.

If there really are spirits on mountains, he thought, then on this mountain, where there isn't another soul to be seen, the

Keeper is God. Who says that a sentinel can't become the spirit of a mountain?

The young Keeper tries to console himself as he sits alone, peering up at the spiralling stone steps that lead to the peak. Each day he wakes hoping to see a visitor on his mountain – a human being, a deer, even a raging wild beast. But not even the wind keeps him company; even the wind is sleeping. Sleeping since the mythical era of Eastern Jin, and still nothing has woken. It is a deceased mountain, he thinks. Why is it even still considered a tourist destination? Why are people still made to pay two yuan to enter its gates?

The young Keeper dozes briefly. He wakes and, between the pillars of the third pavilion, he watches the sun creep behind a cloud. Again, he dozes for a while, and then, with great effort, lifts his lids slowly. The sun has escaped from the cloud's clutches. He thinks he hears a noise. Could it be the sound of the sun travelling across the sky? It is an unfamiliar sound. Can it be a person, a visitor on his mountain? The mountain keeper opens his eyes even wider: it's a woman. A blue sun hat covers her face. She is breathing heavily as she climbs the steep steps. Bless Buddha, a woman! Oh, let her be a good-looking young woman. And if she's wearing skimpy clothes then all the better. The Mountain Keeper silently says his prayers, hopes that he will be given reason to offer thanks at Red Snail Temple. In all his time as guardian of the mountain he has never been inside the temple to pray to Buddha. He hopes he hasn't offended the gods. He feels sudden, slight pangs of regret.

4

As he laments, the guest makes her way up the steps. Her face is shielded from view by that blue sun hat until her eyes come level with his. Oh Buddha, it really is a young woman. With soft hair and a childlike face and bright eyes. She is pretty. She could be wearing a little less but her legs seem slender enough under that skirt. The Mountain Keeper is ecstatic. The day could conjure nothing else to make him happier. The reason for his entire existence becomes clear to him as the young woman walks past, tantalisingly close.

Clip, clop, clip, clop. She keeps on walking, straight past him. She doesn't lower her eyes for a second, as if she's being pulled up the mountain by an invisible kite flying high in the sky. She passes him as if he is a rock; a rock with no feeling and no story. She takes off her sun hat and mops her sweaty brow. Then she raises her head to look up to the very top of the mountain, and starts to climb again. It's as if she's forgotten there's anything but sky in the world.

The Mountain Keeper turns his head and stares, horrified, at the clambering woman's back. It's the first time all day he's turned his head to look up. Well, when there's no one there, what is there to turn your head for? There is nothingness at the top of the mountain. There is only down, down the mountain to the city, to Beijing.

A freak gust of wind blows up the valley, bending the mountain's pines and bamboos into an enormous crescent wave. Fearful, the Mountain Keeper looks up at the thin body above him. She sways fiercely and her hat hangs in the air then slowly surfs across the sky away from her. The young woman stops dead as if the wind is calling her back. She drops to sit on the stone stairway and gazes down the mountain. Her pale face shadowed by a passing cloud. Another gust of wind brushes past her. She suddenly starts to cry. The mountain is desolate, the wind strong. He can hear her sobs. He is shocked.

The Mountain Keeper hides himself in the darkness of the pine trees. He doesn't want to let the crying visitor see him. On that paralysed mountain, on Red Snail Mountain with its Red Snail Temple but no monks and no red snails, he watches her sitting there, crying alone. And he is bemused. But what can he do? He's just the man who watches over the mountain.

By the time the wind has dropped, she has gone. The wind steals her cries too. But why has she come to his mountain? Is she a tourist? Why has she paid two yuan to climb to its peak? Maybe she was at the temple burning joss sticks and then decided to climb to the summit at the last minute. But why is she alone? Why is she alone on the top of the mountain crying? And why didn't she say anything to him? Maybe he could have comforted her. Maybe if she'd seen him she wouldn't have cried. The Mountain Keeper considers notion after counter-notion, and looks skywards as the setting sun slips beneath his shoulders.

His thoughts abruptly turn panicky; what if something has happened? He stands up and looks down the rocky stairway – no one. He runs to the northern slope and starts down in fright, checking the undergrowth as he goes and occasionally glancing up at the overhanging tree branches. Each time he comes to a cliff edge he stretches his neck over the precipice to make sure there are no bodies in the valley.

All the way down he sees no sign of her.

The Mountain Keeper closes the gate and hangs the open lock on its metal frame. He stands there a while as if waiting for someone he knows. When the second gust of wind blows the bamboos, he puts the key in his pocket and turns away.

When the Mountain Keeper wakes the next morning his eyelids are heavy, his hair is full of sand. The sun is much brighter than it was yesterday. It's an effort for him to put a shirt on and walk out of his house. He feels aged somehow. Overnight things have changed. He senses that he feels something but he can't recognise what it is. And there is the woman. Woman, he murmurs to himself, is an impossible being. He stands there surveying his place. Mountain remains mountain, dirt remains dirt and peak remains peak. A rose-coloured cloud is floating towards him, he feels like he has become one of the mountain's many solitary rocks. He looks up at the mountain's peak, imagining the same young woman from yesterday sitting in the shade of the third pavilion. She dries her tears with her sleeves. Then she raises her head, peering down at the mist floating through the bamboo trees. The Mountain Keeper thinks of the lonesome temple abandoned in the woods. Suddenly, he feels like going down there to pray, to pray for his mountain.

WINTER WORM SUMMER WEED

A young Tibetan sits on the sand by Zha Ling Lake. He is skinny, about eighteen, with a buffalo-skin satchel hanging from his bony shoulder. The throbbing sun scorches his thick dark hair. The dreamlike lake is silent before him, a steely blue. The Kunlun Mountains reach up beyond the lake, iced snow coating the tops, peak after high peak.

The boy is from Maduo County in Qing Hai Province. His name is Guo Luo. In the summer he climbs the mountains to harvest famous herbs known as Winter Worm Summer Weed. He is a professional Winter Worm Summer Weed gatherer. This herb is well known for its nourishing and beneficial properties, but actually the plant starts out as an insect. In winter it is a caterpillar, a Winter Worm. Come summer, the caterpillar has died and its remains are absorbed by the earth, becoming a worm-like herb that looks like a strange weed. This is ground up and used in medicinal soups and tonics.

Even people who don't use traditional Chinese medicine will use it in their Sichuan hotpot, boiling it in the dregs of spicy chilli soup. Its exact merits are unclear, but it is thought to improve the flow of your chi, the balance between your yin and yang, between the cold and the fire in your bodies.

At the end of summer, the highland snow comes quickly to the mountainside, and Guo Luo can no longer gather the herbs. Instead he travels across the county's vast sand pastures and catches rats.

People eat rats in Maduo County. Stir-fried with coriander and ginger. Guo Luo can make a handful of yuan to survive by selling a summer's worth of herbs and a winter's worth of rats.

Other young men like Guo Luo, weathered and thinned by the sun, squat by the edge of the lake. Their fingers gently fondle the recently collected herbs. They watch old fishermen hauling their catch onto the decks of the boats. Wooden notices are staked out around the lake, put up by the local government. Big red characters warn. 'This lake is government property. Fishing is illegal.'

But these fishermen pretend they can't read. And maybe they can't, who knows? There is always someone fishing, even in broad daylight. It says it's illegal, but the local officials don't bother them. Who would listen, anyway? If you live on the mountain, you eat from the mountain. If you live by the water, you eat from the water. How else can one live?

The people living in Maduo County were originally nomads. When they first came to this place, the lands by the mountains and the lake were vast fertile grasslands. But their herds grazed so much that now there is no grass, only sand and dead roots. The land has become a desert, a rat-infested desert. Rodent holes appear every three steps, and whole colonies every five. The rats burrow underground and feed on the remaining roots of grass. The locals complain about the rats, blaming them. 'The rats have decimated the plateaus.' Guo Luo and the other herb gatherers kill them – it can even be fun. He doesn't have a professional weapon, he'll grab any nearby stick to kill the rats. Locals use rat skin to make bags and cases. In restaurants, chefs have four ways of cooking rat: braised in soy sauce, heavy-fried, steamed, or stir-fried in a smoking wok with red chillies and spicy salts. A mouthful of rat can be as tender as the best beef fillet.

Tibetan is Guo Luo's native tongue. He has learnt Mandarin and even picked up some English from tourists who travel to the lake with the beautiful mountain landscape. His features are delicate, his face almost feminine despite the sunburnt skin. His eyes are bright. He moves like a little prince of the mountains. When he climbs the mountains with the others, it is always Guo Luo who returns with the most herbs. It is as though the weeds offer themselves up to him, begging to be taken. His reputation is such that when Guo Luo descends the mountain, buyers are waiting by the lake to ask his prices. Middlemen buy the herbs in bundles and scurry back to the nearest big city, Xi Ning, where the herbs can be sold to pharmaceutical companies at a profit.

★

As he walks down the mountain Guo Luo carries three bunches of herbs in each hand. His eyes are on the faraway mountaintops, covered with eternally thick snow. It's as though it has never melted, even in all the eighteen years of his life. He pictures the snowline where the white winter lotus used to grow. The white plant was hard to see against the snow. Guo Luo would ride his horse up the mountain to pick the lotus and then sell the flowers to the government pharmacy in the local town. Now the lotus has almost disappeared, picked to extinction. No point riding up to the snowline now.

He stands still, empty and drifting in the afternoon, bored. Every afternoon is like this – the same clouds, same lake, same mountains. He pulls his eyes back from the mountain to the road below. He can make out rows of white hats, a green flag flapping at the lead. A tour group is coming.

At the head of the group is the female tour guide from Maduo Tourism Bureau. She is about thirty but wears her hair as if she were younger, in a girlish ponytail. Her chubby curves stretch against a tight pink sweater, her body like an overripe pear tree laden with blooms. She is sweet to Guo Luo as if he were her younger brother. Each time she brings tourists to the lake, she lets him know what to expect. 'There is business coming, Guo Luo. They are crazy for the herbs.' This time the group is from Singapore; the last lot were Japanese. She tells him to raise his prices. 'They're superstitious, they know this county has the best Winter Worm Summer Weed herbs.'

Guo Luo watches her usher the crowd of white hats towards him. He tilts his chin up to the sky and whistles.

A scurry ensues, like a pack of rats descending, as his herb-picking companions flock from every direction. The tourists are a group of middle-aged women with money. You know the kind. Fearful of robbers, they carry their money in black leather wallets around their necks, cheap purses strung with shiny silver and gold chains. On this occasion, Guo Luo and the boys do very well.

The tourists stop coming at the end of the summer. The snow quickly covers the mountains. There is no autumn here, and Guo Luo has no work as the herbs are buried deep under the thick snow. He wanders around, nothing but sand and rats and occasional clumps of ugly flowers shaped like steam buns. The rats move like Guo Luo – they scurry impulsively from one hole to another. He hits them at random. He doesn't know what to do with the coming winter.

One day the female guide reappears, even though it is nowhere near tourist season. She is excited, her cheeks are rosy.

'I have good news! I'm being transferred to the Tourism Bureau in the city, and the bureau said I could have an assistant. Do you want to come and be my assistant?'

Guo Luo is slow to react. He tightens his hat, as if to help him gather his thoughts.

'So I guess we won't see you much around here any more.'

The guide stands on the parched and shrivelled former grasslands, her eyes full of expectation, like a lone wispy cloud hoping for rain.

'Don't you want to live in the city, boy?'

'The city of Xi Ning?'

'Yes. You could work as a guide in the Tourism Bureau there, and could drive the coach for us.'

Guo Luo says nothing. He cannot even imagine what she describes. The female guide watches him.

'What are you thinking? What do you think about all day?'

Guo Luo doesn't answer. He takes a peek at her two round breasts, as though hoping he might find some Winter Worm Summer Weed hiding there.

'If it's girls, I could introduce you to one or two.'

'It would have to be a city girl,' Guo Luo finally says.

'Why?'

'City girls can pay the right price for my herbs.'

The female guide keeps still, but suddenly she is like a bloom that has lost its freshness, wilted. Her eyes reflect the landscape around them, the grassland without any grass.

Guo Luo looks back at the mountain, its sides already encased in snow. He wishes he could be on the mountain right now, gathering his herbs. The female guide moves away, disappearing into the sandy landscape. Guo Luo watches her go. Cities, girls, what does it matter? He mutters to himself and turns back to the mountain.

The Winter Worm Summer Weed lives on these mountains. Winter Worm feeds the mountainside, and the mountain feeds us. We live from the mountain, live from the Winter Worm Summer Weed. We are Winter Worm Summer Weed people, that is all.

BEIJING'S SLOWEST ELEVATOR

1. The Darkness

At night, owls fly out from their caves. They can't see what's close to them, but their eyes penetrate the deep darkness. I too am a creature of the night. I like to think that I'm an owl, an owl that flew from South China to Beijing.

During the day, I am a motionless lump of flesh in a bed. Leaving the city to roar outside, my head is heavy on the pillow, my conscience sinks into a dark forest inhabited by far-sighted owls. Some days I cannot sleep so I sit in the kitchen, letting the time pass. I leave my flat only if I need to eat something. Then, I walk on the shadowy side of the bright street, my head down like a sunflower at night. I don't want to meet anyone's gaze, I only see shoulders and feet pass by, one after another. I don't want men that I've met in the karaoke parlour I work in to recognise me. They too would feel embarrassed to see me in broad daylight. Yes, I am a karaoke mistress. I comfort men during their long nights. With my voice, and sometimes with my body too.

2. The Elevator

I wake up at noon, my throat burning. The city heat is filling my mouth, dust covering my eyes. Beijing is a desert. How could an emperor ever want to build a capital in such a dreadful place? I wonder. The raging heat of the summer is unbearable, and in the winter, it's freezing to death. People come here purely to make money; the rest is punishment. And I follow in their footsteps. I know. Only money matters.

Money, the bastard. I drag my thirsty body to the kitchen, open the fridge in search of relief. The watermelon I bought yesterday is finished, and there isn't a single bottle of water, only some ice sitting bored in the freezer. You can't drink Beijing's tap water. Putting on a pair of slippers, I leave the flat.

I spit. This must be the slowest elevator in Beijing. I wait endlessly, listening to the clunky engine in some distant dark hole, loading and unloading people. The building has thirty floors and two hundred households, and there's just one elevator. One elevator! What stupid architect thought of this?

The doors open abruptly. In the middle of the crowd, I see the young man from the thirtieth floor. He is wearing a sky-blue shirt and denim trousers — he always wears trousers, even on the hottest days.

I try to squeeze into the elevator.

'Excuse me…'

'There is no room,' somebody moans.

'There is room,' the young man from the thirtieth floor says.

The door shuts, his eyes briefly brush over me, and I look away at the mirror. He's tall, with a dreamy face, or a face of melancholy. His manners make me think of a Tang Dynasty scholar poet, pure and elegant, resting by the banks of the Yangtze River, contemplating the distant moon. It's not often you come across someone like him in Beijing. Here, both the city and its inhabitants are trapped in a heavily polluted air.

I turn round; our eyes meet for a second. His smile is so subtle that I wonder if I only imagined it. I turn towards the mirror again, looking at myself. I hardly ever notice anyone in my building apart from him, and we usually meet in the elevator. A couple of times I have seen him carrying cat food. What colour is his cat, I wonder – black? White? Black and white?

Then all of a sudden, warning words echo in my ears: 'There is no real love in this city. Keep your distance from that temptation.' The girls in my karaoke parlour tell me, 'Your body is your most valuable asset; your body pays your wages.' In my business, we girls must be armed at all times: do not believe in love, do not fall for a man, always wear a short skirt and always carry a pack of condoms.

I stop gazing at the man in the mirror; instead I stare at my toes. Someone is smoking in the elevator. Every object is blurred. I feel like I'm standing inside a chimney. I start to cough. Finally, the elevator lands, heavy as a plane. The door opens and I am caught up in the swarm of people rushing through the lobby. I search for the man from the thirtieth floor in the scattering crowd, but he's disappearing into the scorching sun – the world blurs; everything turns white in the summer light.

3. The Skin

It is five in the afternoon. I am sitting on my plastic chair at my plastic kitchen table, finishing a bowl of congee. I've already gobbled half a tin of pickled cucumbers. The sour and salty taste remains in my mouth, and my body feels much happier. I like this peasant food. Congee and pickles were my staple diet when I was a kid – it was what our whole village ate. You don't find food like this in my karaoke parlour.

Leaving the dirty dishes on the table, I start to put on my make-up as the sky begins to darken. If there is something I don't like about myself, it's my skin. I have soil-coloured skin, brown, like a true peasant. I grew up in the middle of paddy fields in the south, my family owned two buffalos and some pigs, and I've been exposed to the sun's glare ever since I was born. Pale skin is an unattainable fantasy for us; only true city people can afford that silky white skin. The man from the thirtieth floor, he's got all the features of a born city boy – white complexion, practised speech and a clean vocabulary, and he is tender and restrained. He's not some foul-mouthed, black-toothed entrepreneur who makes his money selling pigs' feet to illiterate peasants at inflated prices and goes to karaoke parlours to have fun with girls.

It's almost six in the evening. Through the window I can see the street lights start to shine, one after another. Putting on a pair of high heels, I lock the door and wait for Beijing's slowest elevator to take me out into the night world.

4. The Karaoke

Jukebox to Heaven is the karaoke parlour I work in. It is near the Beijing Olympic Park. It's not bad, I have to say – a couple of years ago, there wasn't a single shop around there, but now: three gyms with swimming pools and saunas, B&Q, Tesco and Carrefour, one after another, built like military bases. The young middle class spend plenty of time here every day. Cars leave with piles of products every minute. People desperately want to spend their money. Maybe they think that's the most effective way to feel alive.

My shift starts at seven, and my taxi route to work is past a huge outdoor car park. Girls like me – young, cheap labourers from the countryside – lean against parked cars or strut around doing deals with the drivers. Summer nights are all right for business, but the winter is tough. I used to be one of them, hunting money in the dark windy streets, but now I sing on a leather sofa, and cocktails are waiting at the bar.

Jukebox to Heaven is fairly large; twenty girls work here, not including the waitresses. We hardly ever see the boss, but

I'm told he is linked to some big name in the government. His main income is from property development apparently. Perhaps he owns half of the Olympic Park – it's not impossible. 'Red mafia', hotshot businessman with a communist background – that's what people say about our invisible boss.

The place I work in is clearly aimed at entrepreneurs – a high-class establishment. I don't really do much here. Mostly, I smile and say sweet things to the men, or sit on their lap, encouraging them to drink the expensive imported liquor. They can pick from five thousand songs in our karaoke collection and sing them in front of a TV screen, from 1940s communist songs to *Titanic* – 'My Heart Will Go On'. And if the man wants more, and has enough cash, then I have to give in. Security are on the watch outside the rooms, fists ready in case anything should get out of hand. Sometimes I get bruised and occasionally I bleed, but I don't complain. I guess there's no easy job in this world. Even the potato farmer has to fear the day when he'll chop off his toe with a mistimed swing of the pickaxe.

5. The Singer

Men's faces always appear old to me. My memory of them gets updated every day. Most of the customers at the karaoke parlour are ageing, with wives and children at home. They're of the generation born during the fifties, who dedicated the prime of their lives to the socialist cause. Sometimes I feel they want to regain their lost youth by treating young women badly, or using them like public utilities. They say to me: 'Bastard! Life is so unfair to us, girl, I tell you. I looked after stinking chicken farms for thirty years, and now I am fifty and I have some spare money to spend on you. Tell me, how are you gonna satisfy me tonight for my thirty years' misery, eh?' Or even worse: 'This is my plan this year: I'm going to divorce my old wife, and have fun for the rest of my life – I'm going to have different girls every week. Why not? I've got money now and you're going to respect me tonight, understand that?'

It is their revenge, perhaps. But why don't I ever get to have fun? I am fast moving towards thirty, and I've never had one day without worrying about money and survival.

It is Monday night, not much is going on. Contracts are still to be negotiated and deals are still being discussed in white office buildings. Bored, I watch a soap on TV with two other girls; it's called *I Fell in Love with a Police Officer's Wife* – it's not too bad. A man walks in. I can't even be bothered to raise my eyes. But he picks me out. I stand up and lead him into the karaoke room he's hired, handing him a menu on the way.

He orders some Bordeaux wine. There is no Chinese wine on the list – too cheap. Instead of talking, the man starts to study my face. I realise he is surprisingly young, about thirty, and he doesn't seem too confident about having his hands in my lap.

And then he says: 'You know what? I think that…you look like a classmate of mine.'

I give him a smile. 'Sure. Was she cute?'

'Yes she was … But really, you look just like her.'

I spit on the carpet. 'Come on! There are millions of girls in this city with my kind of looks.'

He carries on studying me as he takes the wine glass from my hand. I'm getting nervous, there is indeed something familiar about his face, as if it comes from an old dream. No one knows who I really am; nobody is allowed to know that.

'You definitely look like someone I used to know,' he insists. I turn away towards the TV and change the channel at random. 'Excuse me for asking, but where are you from?' he goes on.

Where am I from? That accent is so familiar. I begin to realise where he is from, and I start to panic. From the corner of my eye, I glance at him − I must have known this man in my former life, back home. My mind starts to reel, searching for ways to escape his questions, to make up a story. I'll say I'm from a tiny unknown town in Shan Dong or in Hu Nan Province, something like that.

But he doesn't wait for my answer and says the dreaded words: 'Are you not Zhang Yan?' I am lost. I pretend I have never heard that name before. Impatient, he carries on. 'Your home town is Jiu Long, in Fu Jian Province, right?'

He knows my past. I cannot escape. Trying to sound cool and casual, I reply: 'You must be mistaking me for someone else, mister. You're too drunk.'

'No way! I am totally sober!' he protests angrily. 'You are Zhang Yan from Jiu Long primary school and I am your former classmate, Ma Yue San.'

My eyes leave the TV screen and look at his face, trying to

21

recall my old classmate. It's true, this man really does look like Ma Yue San. Ma Yue San from Jiu Long primary school. I remember he was good with numbers and always got top grades in our maths tests.

'I don't know what you're talking about, mister. I am from Si Chuan Province, so I can't be your schoolmate,' I say.

'So you have a twin sister then?'

I turn the TV up louder; a Hong Kong song covers his voice.

'Sorry, mister, I don't care about your classmate. The only thing I care about is making you feel good. Shall we have another drink? Do you have enough money for this?'

'I haven't made my millions yet. But I'm not poor – we design anti-virus software that sells all over the country.'

'Anti-virus software, huh?' I repeat, trying to think of something to say.

'Yes. We just bought a building on the 4th Ring Road.' He pauses, scrutinising my face again. He sighs and then continues. 'Aiyah. You don't want to admit who you are. But I have a good memory…'

He's got a good memory, but I've got a thick skin, and I don't let the world upset me, particularly when it comes to men. But this time, my schoolmate's rambling has unsettled me. If the people in Jiu Long knew how I made my living, I wouldn't ever be able to return home. Zhang Yan works in a state-run factory in the capital. And she has a good boyfriend who works with her. This is what my parents know. I can feel a tingle of anxiety creeping down my spine. I must shut up Ma

Yue San. I'll drown his brain in liquor and make sure that when he crawls out of bed tomorrow morning, he'll have no memory of his schoolmate Zhang Yan working in a karaoke parlour. Besides, nobody here knows my name. Here, I am Ai Lian – Lotus Lover – a name men like to spend a night with. There has never been a Zhang Yan at Jukebox to Heaven, never.

And so after a few songs by Faye Wong, the Bordeaux is finished. I persuade him to order some whisky, the most expensive thing on the menu – the boss always tells us we should get the men to order it. We drink Scotch until Ma Yue San is soaked in it. Twice already I've gone to the toilet; my throat is raw. I learnt the trick from the other girls: when you drink a lot, stick your fingers down your throat and vomit it up again; it's the only way you can last the night. After my third trip to the toilet, I taste a trickle of blood dripping down my throat. But that doesn't matter right now – my mission is to persuade Ma Yue San to drink even more and to sing karaoke with me.

My classmate has passed out on the sofa, as dead as a drunken shrimp. I think I don't need to worry any more. I go back to the counter, write down the list of what he's drunk, and tell the waiter that he'll pay in the morning. Then I return to the reception room and drink some tea while waiting for my next customer.

6. The Paddy Fields

Four in the morning. Sitting alone under a neon light in a windowless room, I reach for the remote control and mute the TV. The sound of laughing and singing comes from every corner. I am tired. My only other customer tonight was an overweight businessman from Hu Nan with a coarse drawl that reminded me of old videos of Chairman Mao. The weight of his enormous body made me choke, and as I lay under what seemed like a ton of stale sweat and beer, the tang of sour vomit seeped back into my mouth.

I drink a cup of green tea, then another, and then another. I start to feel better. Ma Yue San's words are still ringing in my ears. I'm hungry. I miss the south. I miss a bowl of congee and the smell of boiled rice. An image of rice fields spreads out before my eyes, covering the vast horizon of Beijing. Water buffalo grunt in the mushy fields; my parents, in straw hats, crouch down to plant rice sprouts, their feet wet and muddy in the water. In the middle of the field a lanky scarecrow wards off the sparrows, during harvest time in the summer, straw stacks are piled on the hills to dry. The wind is warm and fermented. I can smell the grain, the soil, the grass, the sweetness of those fields, the fields where I grew up with my classmates and played with my friends. These high heels hurt my feet. I look at the dim carpet, the red neon illuminating my skin. I feel like crying.

7. The 4th Ring Road

At six in the morning, I leave Jukebox to Heaven and flag down a taxi.

The journey home at dawn is my favourite part of the day. Sitting in the taxi I watch the hushed and naked city wake up. The smell of freshly-cooked breakfast, half-awake children pulling on their satchels and beginning their journey down the street towards school. Construction workers pouring sand onto the street, lines of workers pedalling towards distant factories. But I am not in a rush, my duty is done. There are no more ageing entrepreneurs to entertain. I am on my way home where, at last, I will sleep, alone.

8. The Conversation

As the taxi draws up at my place I notice someone sitting at the entrance of the building. The figure is hunched and dishevelled. As the driver pulls up I realise it's the man from the thirtieth floor, or rather, a jaded version of him. Who is he waiting for at this time? His chin is stubbly, his face is sallow as if he hasn't slept.

He looks up as I walk towards him, but this time there is no welcome in his eyes, and no cat food in his hand either. I can hear the elevator clunking up and down. 'Are you OK?' I can see he feels uncomfortable.

'I can't get in.'

'Lost your keys?' I ask. He doesn't reply. 'Well, doesn't someone else have a set?'

After a while, he answers: 'My keys are with my girlfriend…' I'm annoyed. What do I care about his girlfriend and his keys?

'Can't you get them from her?'

He shakes his head. Without thinking, I sit down next to him. He recoils slightly, but that doesn't bother me. We sit there in silence for a while. I look up at the sky. It is a clear morning, smoky blue without any clouds. I notice he looks at the sky too. In the end, he says: 'We split up last night. And when I got home, I realised I'd left my keys at her place. I can't go back though.'

So did he spend the whole night miserably sitting on those stairs while I was drinking whisky with a classmate from back home? But then it strikes me – he is single after all. I think this city needs more unattached single people like him.

My enthusiasm spills out. 'If you want, come up to my place. You could call the caretaker, and ask him to help you get in. Then you could get a new key made or something.' He doesn't answer. When he eventually stands up, I take that as a yes. I tug on his sleeve like a sister, and lead him to the elevator. On our way up, I examine his face and decide he looks the same age as me – maybe twenty-five or twenty-six. He could be a good father.

9. The Congee

A few minutes later, the man from the thirtieth floor is sitting on the plastic chair in my kitchen, staring at the half-eaten dish of pickled cucumbers and the bowl of leftover congee from yesterday. He hasn't spoken a word since we came inside. He must think it's strange to eat congee and preserved vegetables. Young city people don't eat things like that. I pour him a glass of mineral water; he takes a sip. Still silent. His eyes are moving around the room, and I know what he must be thinking: Does this woman really live alone in this big flat?

I break the silence. 'Would you like some congee? I made it yesterday.'

He nods vigorously. I'm surprised; maybe he hasn't eaten, maybe his tearful battle with his girlfriend has left him starving. Or maybe he's just being polite. Who knows?

I fill a bowl with congee from my rice cooker, heat it in the microwave, then fish some pickled cucumbers and spicy cabbage from a jar. I place this humble food in front of him. He takes the chopsticks and eats. He makes surprisingly little noise for someone eating so quickly and with such relish. I sit down beside him and admire his appetite. I've never watched a city boy eat congee before, and as I study him now I decide that he seems to be a good man – he eats with such an honest manner – something I've only seen in my village people until now. I trust his manner.

As he starts a second bowl, I walk through to the bedroom to change. I put on a loose T-shirt and a pair of cropped jeans.

27

I wish I had never worked in Jukebox to Heaven, I wish I had spent the last few years at university, clutching a pile of books and a violin case.

In the kitchen, a pair of chopsticks rests across the rim of his bare porcelain bowl. He looks content and stands up from my plastic chair.

'Here I am sitting in your chair and eating all your food,' he says. 'And I don't even know your name.'

This is the most perfect moment, I think. He doesn't need to know my name.

He looks at me with questioning eyes. His face is less sad than before. I intend to say my name is Zhang Yan, but my mouth is too quick and the trained words just come out: 'My name's Ai Lian.'

'I'm Li Xin,' he says. 'As you know, I live on the thirtieth floor.' His eyes are smiling again. 'I should go. I've troubled you enough already.'

'But…where are you going to go?'

'I'll see if I can find the caretaker, as you said. Maybe he can force the door.'

Of course, and there also is a cat waiting for him to return – if it hasn't been taken away by the girlfriend.

And then he's gone. I can hear the hum of the elevator moving slowly closer, and then the thud and clunk as the doors open. 'Thanks again, Ai Lian,' says an echo. I'm not used to men thanking me in Beijing. When you sell your body for money, they say, you don't get any thanks.

I sit down in the chair he's just left, warm from his body,

and gaze at the empty bowl. Some grains of moist rice are stuck to the thin end of the chopsticks. The room is quiet; the sun is climbing up my shoulder. Outside, the city is starting to boil. I pick up his chopsticks and put the tips in my mouth. The pungent, sweet aroma of congee fills my senses.

10. The Cat

I've been sleeping all day. A deep and peaceful sleep, like an owl in a forest under the cover of moonlight. I dreamt of water buffalo again, walking slowly in the fields, in the intense heat of my southern province, swinging their tails to chase away the mosquitoes.

When I wake up, the sun is already setting behind the skyscrapers. The city is preparing itself for evening. I hear a knock at the door. Or maybe it's at someone else's flat? I stay in bed a little longer to be sure. The tapping is soft and hesitant, but it doesn't stop. As I slowly get out of bed, I glance at the clock – 6.45 p.m. I'm going to be late for work.

My heart skips a beat as I open the door. It's the man from the thirtieth floor. He has shaved and changed into a clean shirt. A large suitcase in one hand, his other hand wrapped around a cat. A black cat, with glistening eyes like an eagle.

'Sorry to disturb you again,' he says as he puts down his suitcase. The cat tries to jump out of his arms.

'I've had my locks changed.' I nod. 'The thing is, I have to get away from Beijing for a while. Just for a couple of days or perhaps a week. I'm not exactly sure when I'll be back.' I look at his suitcase by the door. He continues: 'I don't know what your thoughts are on cats – maybe you're allergic – but I was wondering whether you could help me look after her for a little while.' I stare at the cat, and it stares at me, with its shiny eyes.

'I...I have no problems with cats,' I answer.

'If you don't like her...I can ask someone else to take care of her.'

I reach out and pull the cat's supple body towards me. Its soft fur warms my chest. 'No problem. I'll look after her,' I say in a clear voice as the cat starts purring in my arms. He smiles. He bends down and picks up his suitcase. As if on cue the cat leaps from my arms and saunters into my apartment.

'Thank you, Ai Lian. I'll be back in Beijing soon.'

I stand in the doorway until the whirr of the elevator fades out, then I go back into my apartment in search of the runaway cat. I walk around the kitchen – just the same chairs and the same table. I enter the living room, but she's not there. The bathroom is empty too. I arrive at the bedroom, and there she is, sprawling on my pillow like someone returning home after a long and tiresome trip.

As I stand by my bed, I gaze at the black animal. Her entire body, from the tip of her ears to the end of her glistening tail, is caught in a beam of the quickly disappearing sun.

'Welcome,' I tell the creature of darkness. 'My name is Zhang Yan, will you come and sing karaoke with me?'

LOVERS IN THE AGE OF INDIFFERENCE

All morning he has been following her. He gazes at her naked shoulders, her hair, her slender bare legs under her shorts. And she knows that he is following her. She knows it so well she doesn't even turn round. She feels angry at him, but at the same time she wants him to grab her, to take her in his arms and hold her.

She walks along the Yangtze River. The river is calm in the summer noon, but turns sharply along its banks as it flows. She has known this city since she arrived here from her village. The river is her place. It is where, during the long and lonely nights, she kills her boredom. But at this time of day, a few boys, eight or ten years old, are swimming in the muddy yellow water, completely naked. They bury their young and innocent bodies under the water, only their wide curious eyes watching her pass. And the man is still following her.

Last night they had sex for the first time. The scene is engraved on her body and her mind. She is a hair salon girl at a hairdresser's on Gong Jian Road, he is a hitman working for the local mafia. He came to her hair salon not to have his hair cut but to get a massage. There was another, prettier girl there but he chose her. He sat on the chair, quiet, observing her in the mirror, as she massaged his head. She could tell he was a troublemaker; she had heard he made his living by attacking and threatening people,. but in her mind she accepted him. Rough but simple, just a peasant man from Henan Province, a village even poorer than hers. Back home, he told her, he used to sell his blood – much more dangerous. 'Thousands of people now have HIV,' he said, watching her.

And they made love – or maybe love is not the right word. On top of her he was savage and violent, as if a war was raging between them. But in the darkness, she felt love. She sensed a strong force overtaking her, from that man, silent and physical, who was bringing her to a place where, possibly for the first time, she felt clearly her own emotion. She was weak, perhaps – she never knew what to make of her future, but she did realise that she had to do something, something dangerous, to mark her youth in a world where vague dreams only come and go.

Then he came. Perhaps, during the sex, he loved her, but when he woke up in the morning he had forgotten that love. Hastily, he grabbed some money from his trousers and threw it at her, 'Go buy a nice skirt, eat a good meal – whatever,' he said carelessly as he tossed three hundred yuan at her. And she was shocked, as she lay on his bed; her heart suddenly dropped. She thought he had felt something for her, a little at least. She slipped on her blue bra. 'I am not a whore,' she screamed, and threw the money back at him. Humiliation. She was soaked in the morning of humiliation.

And instead of leaving her behind and hurrying out the door, he dropped his green army bag, crossed the room and hugged her, surrounding her angry body with his strong arms. He didn't even notice she was crying.

And now she walks and walks along the Yangtze River bank, the sun hitting her hair. She doesn't know what to feel about him. But she knows that he wants her. From the moment she threw the money back at him that morning he suddenly changed, he suddenly realised that she was there – a young woman wanting something more.

He follows her for a long time, perhaps three hours, perhaps four; he is tired, and so is she. At the riverside, a huge ship is waiting to load its cargo. Maybe it will sail to Shanghai, or to Hong Kong, even to Hamburg or Denmark, sitting in the muddy water like a rusty squeaky whale – enormous. And on a small pier jutting out into the river, they stand at the water's edge and watch an old woman bathing a snake in the muddy water, a huge snake about two and a half metres long, like an eel from a fairy tale, with leopard-patterned skin. The woman wears a hat; she doesn't look like the sort of witch who performs tricks with a big snake on a stage. She looks like your auntie next door. The snake seems to be her pet, her best friend, her special creature. Underneath the yellow river water, she caresses her snake and washes it with intense concentration. The snake swims away between the boats, then comes back to her.

The tide is rising, taking over the sandy banks, swallowing the young lovers' feet. Now the snake swims towards him, the mafia hitman, swirling around his ankles, then, gently, it swims up to her.

The horn sounds. Imperceptibly, the boat starts to move, heading east, slowly obscuring the sight. The river is strong, shimmering in the summer heat. They stand, side by side, letting the sun warm their bodies.

JUNK MAIL

From: sfrxxtommj@yahoo.com
To: undisclosed recipient
Sent: 08.07.2009 09:34

Dear friend,

I greet you in name of Our Lord. My name is Mrs Mercy Atteh. I am widow and mother of three girls. I know you think this email embarrassment as we do not know ourselves. I ask you be patient. I feel very pleased to contact you for some assistance and business relationship. I live in Ghana with my children. My husband was loving, caring and hardworking businessman who died in bad car crash. Before sudden death of my beloved husband, he plan business in Kentucky of the United States with 30 million US dollars, but unfortunately he died before.

After his death my husband family say that I can not have his property since I am woman and my children all girls. Well, there are laws here in Ghana which not permit woman to inherit man property, and also I become wife to his brother. Unfortunately to this wicked family, my husband $30 million was put in bank account unknown to his close family. The lawyer is only aware of this money, so I have discuss with a staff of bank I want this money myself so I can take care of my children education needs as my husband family against their education.

Staff of bank say best way to secure this money is transfer to bank account outside of our country, later money be used for business establishment. I ask your sincere assistance in providing us with your bank details to move the fund into your account. As soon as I hear positive response, I provide you with all necessary detail for transfer. However, I decide to give you 20 per cent of total money as gift for assistance and 65 per cent of money for my investment as I will want to keep my husband dream of invest in real estate in Kentucky.

To be able to help me, please send through personal details. Thanking you in advance for your helping response,

Mrs Mercy Atteh

From: sfrxxtommj@yahoo.com

To: undisclosed recipient

Sent: 09.07.2009 16:18

Dear friend,

I am writing to you from Burma, a country in turmoil and at a time of extreme urgency. As you may know, my country is under severe military control and we are oppressed by bad governance and corruption. I am contacting you because I trust you as a civilised Westerner to sympathise with my situation and help my case.

My name is Han Win and I run a local human rights organisation. We have raised about 2 million US dollars over the last several years in campaigning to help the poor people of Burma. But as you know, the government prevents us from saving money so we cannot keep this money in Burmese banks and therefore I ask for your assistance in this matter.

We will need your bank account details in order to transfer the money to you. This way we can be sure that this money is in safe hands and can aid those people in desperate need in our country.

I am sure you will realise that your help not only benefits our organisation but helps the nation as a whole.

Yours,

Han Win

From: sfrxxtommj@yahoo.com

To: undisclosed recipient

Sent: 10.07.2009 13:56

Dear friend,

Please don't feel too surprised that I am writing to you from Russia. My name is Anna Ivanovna Petroshky and I am a woman of 26-years-old. I have been married for 3 years but my loving husband died of a plane crash on the business trip to Turkey.

You may ask why I am contacting you and telling you my personal story. I have known you from the Internet surfing and I believe you are the good person I will be able to trust.

I am contacting you because after my husband died he left me about 50 million US dollars. And as he was involving in some sensitive business in Russia, I dare not to save this money in a Russian bank. And also my late husband's business partners have been trying to access those moneys. Therefore I am contacting you by hoping you can assist a young and vulnerable widow. If you feel you can help me, please contact me and I can send you my photos so you know what I look like. And if you like me and trust me, I can fly over to your country, then you can provide me your bank details in person.

Yours sincerely,
Mrs Anna Ivanovna Petroshky

From: sfrxxtommj@yahoo.com

To: undisclosed recipient

Sent: 11.07.2009 08:09

Dear Respected One,

My name is Mrs Nenita Villaran. I am the widow of the
esteemed former Minister of Finance in the Philippines who died
on 15 May 2002. My husband fell ill here and was flown to
France for treatment but later died in hospital. I cried beside his
dead body for three days and three nights until my body was
dry of tears. On his death I inherited a total sum of 12 million
US dollars from him. The money is currently in a safety deposit
box and held by a security and finance company here in the
Philippines.

Due to the instructions I laid down as conditions when I
deposited the box with the security company – requiring the
maximum safety possible – no person nor government
organisation can trace the whereabouts of the box until I am
ready to claim it. For this reason the security company has
used their diplomatic means to send the box out of the
Philippines to the Côte d'Ivoire where they have an
underground secret vault. This deposit was coded under a
secret arrangement as a family treasure.

My main purpose of sending you this email is because I find
you a trustworthy person and I wish to entrust you in shipping
the box of money to any address that you think is secure and

safe in France. We can talk soon about your percentage of the money saved.

Unfortunately my husband's family has successfully collected all his property; and they haven't even stopped at that – they have told me to surrender all bank account details to them. My future and destiny rests upon the contents of the safety deposit box in the Côte d'Ivoire so I would never give up that information to them. Out of fear of my husband's family, and because the situation has now become uncontrollable thanks to pressure from the government of the Philippines, I decided to look for a trustworthy person who could assist me in retrieving this box of money from the security company for onward lodgement into his account for the purpose of future investment.

I ask you honestly to consider my situation seriously and come to my aid. I have discussed my decision with the security company and they have agreed to dispatch this consignment to you in your country by diplomatic courier. Please contact me urgently with your personal details upon your acceptance so that we can discuss how to go about this transaction speedily.

Thanking you in anticipation,
God blessing,
Mrs Nenita Villaran

From: sfrxxtommj@yahoo.com

To: undisclosed recipient

Sent: 12.07.2009 06:04

Gretings from Mrs Lee,

I feel luky when world is not as I thawt. I go thru yor profile thru intnet i decid contact you for frendship and asistents for distribushon of my inherentents. My name is Mrs Jenny Lee. I am dying woman in Malasia. I deside to donat to you and yor church in Losan in Switzland. I have 70 years old and I am cancer, and I lived alone for 10 years and I feel lonly. But now dying woman lIke me I am happy to meet God in the place where I supoze to meet Him.

I deside donat my wealthy to you for good work of God, not give my relatifs use my funds ungodly. Ples pray that the good Lord forgiv my sin. I have asked God to forgiv me and I believe He has becos He is a mercyfull God. I will be going into the hospital for an operashon in the next 2 weeks from now.

I desided to donat $2,500,000 (two million five hundred thosand dollar) to you for good work of the Lord, and also to help the motherles and less privelege and also for the asistents of the dying person like me. I have ajust my WILL and my lawer is change my will and he is plan transfor of funds from my acownt to you.

I wish you all best and the good Lord bless you, and ples use funds well and alway extend good work to others. I have

41

contact my legal and tell him that I have WILLED
($2,500,000.00) to you and I have also tell him that I am
WILLING that to you for specific good work of charitie. I beleve
you no the hart of God as I do. Thanks and God bless. I will
directiv you after mail from you.

Yors,

Mrs Jenny Lee

From: customerservice@junkfilter.com
To: undisclosed recipient
Sent: 15.07.2009 11:23
Subject: JUNK MAIL WARNING

Dear Customer,

Spam Filter ensures that suspected junk mail is delivered to the
Spam folder, to block your email inbox being polluted from
political and commercial conspiracy emails. These junk emails
will be deleted after one week.

Our Junk Mail Virus Protection detected the virus 'W32.Auraax'
in your files. We scanned these emails using Norton AntiVirus
but were unable to clean it. Please contact us with your FULL
IDENTITY AND PERSONAL DETAILS AS WELL AS YOUR CONTACT
DETAILS, so we can assist you preventing future junk mail.

Thank you,

Junk Mail Customer Service

THEN THE GAME BEGINS

The man who invented mah-jong is a hero. Yeah, definitely a hero. He saves people's lives, people like me who have nothing good to count on at night. You know, I used to think that playing mah-jong was only for grandparents, and a young woman should have better things to do. But now I know this game is for *everyone*, for all the people in China. I wonder what Chairman Mao thought of mah jong during the Cultural Revolution – maybe he tried to stamp it out. Very unwise I think.

I feel a much stronger person since I started playing mah-jong. And you know what else? – it's brought about a romance, an affair.

Let me explain to you why I like gambling – and now gambling with my marriage as well. For the last three years I have spent every day answering phones in my office in a perfect, polite voice, answering every query with a smile, and every evening cooking rice in an empty home, waiting for my husband Hui to walk through the door. God, how boring my life sounds – don't you think? By the time he comes home the dinner I have slaved over for him is cold and unappealing, so I almost always eat alone before him. Then I watch crappy TV on our crappy television set until Hui opens the door, weary as always. He seems to have put on weight recently; I wonder if he's been drinking too much beer after work with his colleagues, or perhaps his cheap shirt is just too tight over his belly? You know, he's not that handsome or special, after all. He's just an ordinary man, I've realised – and, disappointing or not, that's the truth.

You know, I haven't made a single friend in this city of eighteen million people. And why is that? I used to think I was one of the many victims of old Confucius' rules – he says the good virtue of a woman is to belong to her husband; the rest is not worth consideration. I thought I was such a modern woman – hah! What did I know? What stupidity! You know, I started to ask myself why I was even living in this big city with my modern plastic flat, my tired and absent husband. There is a whole city full of possibilities out there, and I was sat here at home watching cheap soap operas day after day. My body was getting old and flabby, my mind loose and lazy – I needed something to shock me into living, really living.

Then one night, I stayed up late listening to a CD, an album by Nick Cave. There's this one song called 'Nobody's

Baby Now'. When I listen to this song, my tears flow out freely. The song tells of a melancholy man, separated from his lover who wears a blue dress with violets across her chest. I played it again and again that night, as if on a constant loop. Then I dried my eyes and made a decision. I decided to give up my young housewife life. I need something to happen for a change, and you know what, even if it causes a small disaster – I'm ready for it, I really am. I also realised that for an ambitious man like Hui, home is a drag, and coming back to spend time with the wife in front of the TV is a waste. I never realised that it might also be a waste for me.

And you know, Hui and I don't have a child. They say if a man doesn't want to have children with you within three years it means he doesn't want to be tied to you *forever*. Forever! Ha! What a ridiculous word. Sod that. I'm not interested in forever any more. It should only be written on mah-jong tiles – passed around casually from person to person.

Now everything has changed. Since I've started playing mah-jong, I get home late, often later than Hui. Only the other day I tiptoed into the flat around two in the morning to find him slumped on the sofa, his tie askew and his dinner half finished on a plate on the floor. The TV was still on – some late-night game show – and the volume turned up violently loud in the silent room.

Usually I play mah-jong with Old Gold and his mates or his clients. Then he drives me home in his big shiny BMW round and round the dark ring roads of Beijing. Sometimes we play in karaoke parlours or bars deep into the night. And sometimes I just sit in Gold's BMW listening to his CD collection. Three weeks ago we were sitting there on the tan leather seats with Bryan Adams singing some sentimental crap – I told him I liked it – and suddenly I realised that Old Gold wanted to kiss me. He was looking at me with his head on one side, his arm draped over the steering wheel, leaning forwards. I knew I had a choice: I could go back to my old life, be the woman waiting at home, or I could let Old Gold kiss me, and maybe even enjoy it. I leaned my head on Gold's shoulder and we kissed. We had sex on the back seat; the leather squeaked and was slippery and sticky next to my naked skin. The car park was so quiet, the night porters wandering around with their white torch beams raised and shining so brightly that I was worried someone might find us.

Did I mention that Old Gold is my boss? My husband Hui has played mah-jong with him and his wife Xing many times; sometimes we even play as a foursome: two happy couples. What a reality show.

I work for Gold's newspaper – the *New Consumer*. For three dull years I was the receptionist and then recently I was promoted. I know that Old Gold noticed me. He used to comment on my dress or new hairstyle, and occasionally, you know, I would find him staring at me while he waited in reception for a lunch guest or client. Now my job is to read Western fashion magazines and to report on the latest trends from Milan, Paris or London. Gold is a smart guy – he knows people in the government and seems to understand how to run a business in Beijing. And of course he was well ahead of everyone when he bought his 250-square-metre flat in fashionable Jian Wai Soho – the most expensive area in Beijing – way before it hit the big time.

One night as I lay on my bed, waiting for my husband to come home, the scenes in Gold's BMW flashed through my mind like a film reel. I was so nervous. That night I had played mah-jong with colleagues in a bar, and Gold had won all of our money. He'd flirted with me outrageously all evening, leaning in close, stroking my bare arm and commiserating with me on my bad luck. It was very late and he'd offered to drive me home. He'd been a little drunk and gloating about his winnings. I hadn't wanted to go home – I knew the life there too well. It bored me now. I wanted excitement and change, risk and adventure, and most of all, you know, I really wanted Old Gold. His body wasn't great and his hair was greasy, but the way he touched me triggered something new.

Three weeks later Gold's wife Xing invites me and my husband to 'build the Great Wall' – that's what she calls mah-jong. Now what can I tell you about Xing? So she picks great tiles...but what is that if not good luck? I can't see that she has any other virtues. She's a fashionable woman who does nothing all day long, except go to the hair salon and shop for famous Western brands. Before marrying Gold, she used to sing in a bar, screeching songs from *Titanic* and *The Lion King* in her whiny high-pitched voice, with the lyrics translated into

Chinese. Actually, her voice isn't that bad, but since she's just been a housewife, she only uses it to order takeaway meals, or to curse Old Gold for not spending enough time with her.

My husband Hui loves playing at Gold's place. He loves Gold's brand-new Automatic Mah-Jong Table – a new gadget that automatically shuffles and arranges the tiles for you. It's very popular because people save time in between each round and they can stay focused on gambling instead.

It's a balmy Saturday evening. I wear my best summer dress – fake Dolce & Gabbana; I imagine it being a bit like the blue violet dress in the Nick Cave song. Hui carries some beers under his arm. Arriving in Gold's residential area, we have to pass through a whole series of security gates and wind our way along a complicated garden path. As we approach Gold's front door, I hear a woman crying. I hesitate, but Hui has already pressed the bell. Too late. Gold opens the door with sunken cheeks, and behind him we see his wife Xing's swollen eyes. The floor is a mess. Broken china plates, hair clips, crumpled old newspapers, ladies' underwear, and Gold's leather bag. You know, right at that moment I wanted to run back home as fast as I could, but Hui walked straight into their kitchen and put the five bottles of beer on the table. He is smiling, trying to soothe the atmosphere.

'What's the matter? You two had a little argument?' Hui asks in his best voice.

'Let me tell you what kind of arsehole my husband is!' Xing sneezes.

My heart sinks. I steal a glance at Gold, but he has buried himself in a big leather sofa, and doesn't look up. He stares at his toes. 'Look what I found in his bag!' Xing fetches a small gift box from the top of the TV set. She opens it. It's a silver necklace with a dangling crystal heart. Then she unfolds a note from inside the box and reads aloud: '"For my darling, happy birthday!"' She looks around at us with wide wet eyes, 'Ha!' She looks at Gold. 'Ha!' The words come out sharp and hard like little bullets.

No one says a word. Gold seems to grow more depressed; Hui looks at me for a couple of seconds and then shifts his gaze back to the angry hostess.

'Happy birthday for my darling! Did you hear? That can't be me! My birthday was a month ago, that day we went bowling. He bought me a jade necklace and *I've worn it ever since!*'

I look at her and sure enough she's wearing a green jade necklace. It sits heavily around her neck – the colour is dull and there is no shine to the stone. I'm getting restless. Does Gold's wife know it's my birthday coming up? And has Hui remembered it this time? Last year he didn't, you know, and I ate a special home-cooked hotpot dish all by myself, waiting two and half hours for him to come home and remember. Anyway, it's next Thursday.

'Where are your guts now? Who is she? Eh?'

'I've told you twenty times, my dear, I bought it for you *then* I found the jade and *I always think jade things suit you best!*' Gold yells.

'Let's leave this business for now, guys.' My good-tempered

husband finds a broom, starts to clear up the floor, as confidently as if this was his own house. 'In my opinion, Xing, you need to trust your husband – I mean, look at how happy we are.' Hui turns to me and grins, his face open and bright. 'I believe he bought that for you.'

Xing seems to withdraw a little from her hysteria. She stops speaking, walks to the sofa and curls up beside her husband. Her legs are close to his – no, actually it looks like she's clinging to him. Her gesture makes me feel very strange. I realise I don't want to be in her place, snuggled up to Old Gold's sausage legs and breathing in his musky smell; but I am glad of our moments in the back of his car.

Hui sweeps everything into a corner. Now, with a light-hearted manner, he unfolds Gold's expensive automatic mah-jong table, and installs it in the middle of the room. From the sofa, Gold and Xing gaze at their guest moving around the room in front of them. What a great husband I have!

'Maybe we should go, we'll come some other time,' I say in a tense voice.

'But you've come *all this way*! You can't possibly leave now!' Gold is nearly begging us.

'Yes, let's forget about this stupid necklace and have some fun!' Hui adds. 'It is Saturday night after all!' He drags Gold and Xing off the sofa. Yes, Hui is right, why we can't enjoy this game? I mean, the game of building the Great Wall together.

We all take our seats around the mah-jong table. I am facing Old Gold. His eyes are lowered and beads of sweat dot his upper lip. Hui presses the button, and at once a bunch of white tiles appear. Automatically they line up into four neat, tight walls.

Gold grabs some notes from his wallet and tosses them on the table. So does Hui. Then Xing follows, with her crab-like fingers. We start with one-yuan notes, as usual. I take out my wallet filled with credit cards, but there's no cash in it. My husband notices this and throws me twenty yuan; you know, I can't help smiling to myself at my sweetly innocent dear Hui.

We arrange our tiles. Xing seems less miserable than before. The mah-jong tiles have a special kind of magnetism which suck her into the game – I know only too well. Gradually, she seems to forget what happened twenty minutes ago. Yet she throws the die like a desperate gambler, hypnotized by disaster.

The first hour passes uneventfully. My husband keeps losing money, and Gold's wife is winning. Neither Gold nor I say much. I make a point of being very attentive to Hui and I can feel Gold's eyes on me as I touch my husband's arm or kiss his cheek. I enjoy Gold's stare.

Then the game grows more intense. Gold's wife bids ten yuan at each round. Hui grows desperate. He has lost nearly four hundred yuan, and the game is not even halfway through. I keep as quiet as Gold, who drinks his beer with a professional gambler's face – motionless and unreadable.

Midnight. The beers are all gone. The two men start to drink er guo tou, the strongest Beijing sorghum liquor, while Xing nibbles at a handful of cashew nuts. I sip my glass of water. The situation has my whole attention: I feel like I'm watching a play enacted in real time, and forget that I'm one of the key players. I peek at Xing: she is totally absorbed by the game. Now she stands up, goes to the kitchen and brings back two pomegranates. She lifts one to her lips and bites into the fruit's hard skin; she hands me the other. I take the pomegranate and put it on the corner of the mah-jong table. I can't eat. Really, how can she eat such a hard fruit in the middle of the night?

Waiting for the machine to shuffle the tiles, the two men chink their glasses and drain the fiery liquor. With pomegranate seeds in her mouth, Xing looks at me with a strange expression. Then she says: 'That silver necklace' – she turns and spits out some seeds onto the floor – 'I know who it's for.'

Gold and Hui freeze and stare at her, glasses in their hands, the dregs of liquor a sweet golden nectar.

I am suddenly uncertain. Bit by bit my resolve is gnawed away by a mouse. The air conditioning is too strong. A chill runs down my spine. My legs prickle with pins and needles. They hang loose from my body like the limbs of a puppet. I feel stuck. I can't move my body at all. What should I do? And where should I look? I pull my eyes away from the scene and glance outside through the double-glazed windows: it's a warm summer evening; a group of old people are sitting under a poplar tree, fans in hand, drinking tea. I wish I hadn't worn this thin dress, this Nick Cave blue violet dress.

The automatic table suddenly gets stuck. It makes a disturbing noise, and starts to click and whine.

No one knows what to say.

'I'm going to bed now, you three carry on.'

Very deliberately Xing rises from her chair, leaves the table, still chewing on the hard skin of her pomegranate.

I let out the breath I've been holding for so long.

Gold watches as his wife disappears down the corridor towards her bedroom, then looks back at the table. Still, he doesn't look at me. What a coward, I think. He would never dare to admit to anyone that he likes me, let alone mention that we now make love in the back of his car after every other mah-jong session. I start to think that maybe I don't know my boss at all. Perhaps today is the first day I have really begun to know him. Then beside me, Hui pours himself another glass and takes a long swig of liquor, his face red and swollen. Silence.

I stare at the untouched pomegranate in the corner of the table. It has pink-and-brown mottled skin, and a dirty white sticker saying Product of Iran.

The three of us sit there waiting for the tiles to be delivered onto the table. But the shuffling machine just goes on clicking, like a dying lobster.

STATELESS

He sits beside a window, utterly indifferent to the planes taking off and landing outside.

Having bought a ticket on the least expensive flight, he now finds himself stuck for three hours in Vienna International Airport. Three hours in transit, and not a single thing to do.

All the other travellers seem in a hurry to be somewhere else. Pulling suitcases or shouldering rucksacks, plane tickets clutched tightly in hand, they are scenery in motion, breakers rolling past him like a brightly coloured tide. Only he remains unmoved. Seated, silent and observant, set against the flowing landscape, he resembles something planted by a window. A still life, or a green, green tree.

He reads no books, peruses no maps, does not wander through the duty free shops or attempt to strike up conversations with his fellow travellers. He simply sits there, as silent as the lone piece of hand luggage beside him.

His hair is black, so closely shorn that it is impossible to tell if it might be curly or straight. His face is clean-shaven, with no hint of a beard. His build is unexceptional, neither tall nor short, fat nor thin. He seems devoid of labels, any and all distinguishing tags. He looks, for all the world, to be a stateless man.

Only his eyes mark him out as different. They are a perfect void.

He has decided to change planes here in Vienna, a city not quite large enough to be considered large, before flying on to Paris. He has no specific goal in mind. Where to go and what to do once he gets there are, for him, open-ended questions. He doesn't plan to stay in Paris long – why should he? He doesn't have a lover or a wife, or any one person on his mind. As for his parents, they divorced long ago. Ever since he was young, he has got by just fine on his own. Always travelling from one city to the next, always moving, always alone… He's already in his thirties, and this is the only life he's known. So perhaps he would say that every day of his life has been lonely. Loneliness, to him, is just a way of life.

He continues to sit, as twilight fades into darkness outside the window and it becomes difficult to see anything. He turns away from the window, away from the planes taxiing along the runway, and begins to scrutinise his fellow travellers. The passing blondes, with their shapely behinds and high heels, don't look to be going backpacking or visiting a branch office in another city. Rather, they all seem to be dashing off to some romantic rendezvous or furtive assignation. Women…

they can be so sweet sometimes, he thinks. He sits in silence, sensing that he has touched upon some faint yet genuine longing.

The pretty women fill the terminal with the tap-tap-tapping of their high-heeled shoes. It is a sound he finds pleasing to the ear, but the way the women walk – heads held high and chests thrust forward – strikes him as cold somehow, indifferent. He watches, too, the solemn men with their rectangular black briefcases, respectable suits and immaculate leather shoes. Most look as if they have come to the airport straight from some large convention hall, or as if they are headed directly to a high-rise penthouse conference suite. And then there are the elderly people, couples mainly, shuffling along in their low-heeled sensible shoes and white sun hats. They move slowly, cautiously, leaning on one another for support. He imagines they're setting off on a sunset tour of East Asia, or perhaps returning from some distant city or foreign country where their sons or daughters have taken up residence. Despite their advanced years, they still manage, by some grace of God, to keep pulling one another along. But not this man, he has been sitting here so long that even God has forsaken him.

Three hours seem a lifetime, and a slow one at that. He falls into a daze that is not quite sleep, but a halfway state between dreams and waking. He can still hear the footsteps of the passers-by, the trundling of wheeled suitcases and the airport loudspeaker announcing flights to and from every city on the globe, but he is suddenly no longer certain which airport he is in, or which city, or which country. He blinks and glances around at the signs that surround him, words in a language he does not recognize. It is only when he glimpses the Vienna Symphony Orchestra CD boxed sets on display in the music store opposite that he remembers where he is.

He opens his eyes, but it is an exercise in futility. Of all these figures hurrying by, none has ever stopped to talk to him, none has any connection to him, and never will. Knowing this, he shuts his eyes. When he opens them again, he sees a little girl in a red skirt standing in front of him. No more than seven or eight years old, she has curly blonde hair and is clutching a rag doll that looks just like her. She loiters about uncertainly, unaccompanied by any adult.

He stares at her, and she stares back.

She passes by so slowly, turning back every now and then to glance at him, that she remains in his field of vision for a very long time. How strange, he thinks, to see a child so young walking all alone through an airport. He flashes her a friendly grin and waves hello. Responding to this sudden surge of warmth, the little girl promptly returns his smile. When she smiles, she is even more adorable, he thinks. A little red flower in a little red skirt.

And in an instant, his heart grows sad flooded with rarely felt, inexpressible warmth, a sudden shower falling on a long-parched northern plain. But the child has already disappeared from view. He stands up, still seeing her little red flower smile, still feeling that bittersweet warmth. Suddenly he feels as if he ought to do something, anything at all. He must leave this line of silent chairs, maybe even get out of this airport.

He leaves the waiting area and passes through the terminal. When he arrives at the gate for his connecting flight to Paris, he discovers that the electronic board is already displaying the departure time for his flight, but there are still forty minutes left before he can board. The last odd forty minutes, he thinks, in a strange and alien land...and how to kill the time? He turns about in circles, trying desperately to think of some things that might help grind down these last forty minutes. He comes up with three.

First: Buy a packet of cigarettes, although he rarely smokes. It doesn't matter what brand. A local Viennese brand might be best, might help him to better understand this place.

Second: Pay a visit to the toilets.

Third: Go into the airport bookshop and flick through some magazines. Even if they're only porno mags, a few pages of interesting pictures ought to help kill ten or twenty minutes, at least.

With this plan in mind, he proceeds to do each of the items in turn. First he buys a packet of cigarettes, and even considers smoking one. Then he visits the toilets. Finally he heads for the airport bookshop. On the way, he spies a familiar sight: a little girl in a little red skirt standing in a nearby corner, crying. A kindly old woman, apparently a passer-by, is standing next to the sobbing girl, attempting to console her. She says something to the little girl in a language he cannot understand. When the child does not react, the old woman glances at her watch, heaves a sigh and leaves, dragging her luggage behind her.

No mistake, it is the same little girl: seven or eight years old, curly blonde hair, red skirt. A little red flower in a little red skirt. Only this time around, the little red flower is drenched in tears.

The man walks toward the flower.

He kneels down before her.

She seems to recognise him, for her crying stops, although she continues to sniffle and sob.

Then, in as friendly a tone as possible, he asks her: 'What's your name?'

English. She does not understand. She looks at him with two moist eyes, and blinks. A little fawn.

Travellers burdened with luggage continue to pass by, but none seems the slightest bit curious about the pair, much less inclined to step forward and claim the child.

If only he could find something in one of his pockets, something fun, a piece of chocolate, a biscuit, a fruit drop, anything. But when he stands up to fumble through his coat and trouser pockets, all he finds are a packet of cigarettes, a lighter, airline ticket stubs and some motley small-denomination notes of various nationalities. Nothing remotely fun or small or cute. Finally, he starts pulling faces for the little girl. He didn't know he had it in him, this ability to entertain.

Although the girl eventually stops crying, she does not laugh. She looks confused, her rosy cheeks stained by tears. Such a melancholy expression for a little girl, he thinks. Taking the child by the hand, the man leads her to one of the chairs along the corridor. She follows him obediently. Over the airport loudspeaker comes the announcement that the flight bound for Paris has begun boarding. Glancing over at the departure gate, the man sees that most of the travellers are now standing, as if they were all bound for Paris. Remembering that he has no checked baggage on the flight, the man takes one last look at the passengers filing onto the plane and decides that he will not be leaving. He will stay here in this airport with this unidentified child. He will stay until… until…

Half an hour later, the man hears his name being called over the airport loudspeaker. The message is repeated several times, and then falls silent.

It is late evening now, and the airport is nearly deserted. Flights in and out are few.

The little girl in the red skirt is no longer crying, no longer sad. She is curled up on the man's lap, fast asleep, her rag doll clutched to her chest, clenched in tiny hands. Poor little dolly.

Where will his next stop be? he wonders. Should he wait until morning and take the child to the Viennese police? Should he help her search, help find out what a little girl was doing all alone in a big airport, and why no parent or guardian has come to look for her? But then again, who is he, exactly? When the police ask him about himself, how will he answer? No visa? Not allowed to leave the country? Deportation likely? He is unemployed and there are clearly problems with his passport. Maybe he ought to forget about the police and just head to Paris. But what to do in Paris? He is only too aware that there is nothing waiting for him there. Stop worrying, he decides at last, as he strokes the little girl's curly hair. No point in worrying. He cradles the child's frail shoulders in his arms and drifts at last into a merciful sleep.

AN INTERNET BABY

The two lovers have made up their mind – Weiming and Yuli will sell their baby on the internet. Everyone loves the internet! This baby saw the light of day only five days ago.

Yuli is still at school, in her first year at Chongqing Technical College. For a girl like her, the scandal would be huge – she would certainly be expelled and lose all the time and money she and her oh-so-devoted parents have invested to get her where she is: on the way to a better life, they hope. She has lied to everyone – the dean of her department, her class and dormitory mates. After struggling to hide her growing belly under a large coat for five months, she finally told everyone she had hepatitis and needed to stay at home for a while to recover. And now, in a shabby clinic in a suburb of Chongqing, she's given birth to a screaming little thing.

Yuli is a determined girl; she will study, get her diploma and start a career in a big city. She certainly will not raise a child now. And she will not let anyone know. At home in her village they take family things too seriously. If they knew she'd given birth to a son, they'd come to Chongqing straight away and do everything they could to persuade her to keep the child. But Yuli's mind is clear – while the baby sucks at her nipples with a small, wet face. She won't keep it.

Yuli's boyfriend, Weiming, has one very simple motive for selling their baby: money. Weiming is from the same village as Yuli. They are childhood sweethearts. As a nineteen-year-old, he's had trouble surviving in this city ever since he left his home town to follow her here. There's no way he can imagine helping Yuli with her college fees, sending money to his poor family back in the village and bringing up a baby at the same time. Not possible. He's already working twenty hours a day, on two jobs: during the day he cleans cars, private ones and government ones, and at night he's the doorkeeper at a karaoke parlour. He only sleeps between 3 and 7 a.m. He's beyond exhausted. He has been exhausted from the first day he arrived in this city; his sight is blurred from lack of sleep and his mind is as foggy as the permanent haze hanging over the Yangtze River. But he understands: to help his girlfriend and his family, he has to work like a donkey. A donkey can sleep while standing up, and Weiming has to learn to do that too. He has no choice. He doesn't complain.

So the young lovers agree to sell their baby on the internet. Yuli has studied computer technology at college, she knows how these things work. What people usually sell online are machines – TV sets, Walkmans, bicycles, cameras, or sometimes banned books. Selling a real baby is not very common.

'But what's so different?' Weiming says. 'Selling a baby is the same as selling a car. The only difference is the price. If China could sell some of its population to the West, then there would be fewer people starving here, and we would all have more money.'

Yuli takes some photos of the baby and chooses the cutest one to put online.

HEALTHY NEWBORN BABY BOY FOR SALE: 8,000 YUAN
CONTACT: 13601 386243

The number is Weiming's mobile phone, given to him for his night job. Although they both know that eight thousand yuan is really much too little money for a healthy baby boy, they reason that most people in the provinces are not rich, and as they are in a hurry to get rid of the baby, asking for a small amount of money could sort things out more easily and more quickly. And Weiming also thinks that his girlfriend can always get pregnant again if this plan works out.

After putting the ad online, Yuli feeds her son some milk and changes his wet nappy. She worries that if they don't sell the baby quickly, she'll miss her end-of-term exam and then she won't get her diploma. And she desperately needs that qualification.

The internet ad proves to be very effective. After just a few hours, the phone starts ringing. The first callers want to know whether the whole thing is just a joke, which makes Weiming shout back at them impatiently. He's got no time to joke about life, he needs money. Sounding like a snappy businessman, he yells that if they're not interested he'll just hang up, while his grumpy boss curses him in the background.

But then a woman with a shaky voice explains on the phone that she's from a seaside town near Qingdao, that she is forty-six years old, her husband had been very ill, that's why they didn't have a child, and now he has just died, and she would like to buy the baby, a boy would be ideal. She sounds nervous.

'Can you pay eight thousand yuan cash in one go?' Weiming asks hastily.

'Yes. But I first need to check whether the baby is really healthy.'

Weiming assures the woman that his boy is very healthy and that he'll call her back after discussing things with his girlfriend. Weiming knows that he shouldn't say yes to the first interested person. Through negotiation, prices can be improved.

A few useless phone calls later, a couple ring from Wenzhou, a rich industrial town in Zhejiang Province. They want the baby as soon as possible. 'We can get on the first morning flight to Chongqing and meet you!' The couple speak on two handsets at the same time. Weiming learns that they run a shoe factory in Wenzhou, that they're wealthy but cannot have children.

'Well, I have some other customers interested. How do you

want to convince me to go with you?' Weiming asks, a clear hint that an auction is on. The couple are astute business-people; they immediately offer double the price to get the boy.

So the deal is done. Weiming will receive sixteen thousand yuan in cash. But he doesn't want the couple to come to Chongqing where he and Yuli live. To avoid any risk of being found out by neighbours, Yuli's school friends or his own colleagues, they agree to meet in a city where no one knows them: Shanghai. The meeting point will be Shanghai's People's Park, the next day at 4 o'clock in front of the park gates.

The couple wrap up their sleeping baby and hurry to the train station to catch the next train to Shanghai. Neither Weiming nor Yuli have taken the train much before, and they are like overexcited children twitching in their seats, eagerly observing every station the train passes, picturing themselves ending up working in Shanghai thanks to those sixteen thousand yuan. From time to time, Yuli feeds the baby, but the moody little thing doesn't appear to like the trip and keeps screaming. Every other passenger hates them. At one point, the conductor even comes up to ask whether they need medical assistance.

After fourteen hours, the young couple arrive, pale and exhausted, in the shiny city of Shanghai. Yuli is deeply impressed. People here are more beautiful, fashionable; the houses are taller and much more luxurious than in Chongqing. But Weiming can't enjoy the new city. He's starving and feels more powerless than ever on Shanghai's busy streets. They enter a wonton restaurant and down two bowls of soup each. Weiming finishes half a roasted duck as well. They eat quickly and silently.

Twenty minutes before 4 p.m., Yuli and Weiming are standing in front of the iron gates of Shanghai People's Park. The baby is crying again, and Yuli rocks him in her arms, wearily, until he falls asleep.

The Wenzhou shoe magnate couple arrive on time. They are both about thirty-five and look more humble than they sounded on the phone to Weiming. He thinks they look even more tired than he does, worn out. But as soon as they see the baby in Yuli's arms, the couple's eyes start to glisten. The woman can't help but scream: 'What a beautiful little boy! How cute! How sweet he is!' Her husband stretches out his stiff finger and touches the baby's red cheeks and caresses his soft hair. He seems to be fond of the boy, too. The woman takes the baby from Yuli. She holds him and starts to feel how a mother feels when her son is asleep in her arms.

The little baby wakes up from his nap. His big eyes stare at the strange woman kissing him, speaking some incomprehensible Wenzhou dialect.

'What about the money then?' Weiming asks cautiously.

The man opens his leather suitcase, takes out a heavy blue plastic bag but doesn't give it to Weiming straight away. Instead he says: 'Let's go into the park, we need to check the baby is as healthy as you say.'

It is May; the willows are green, the bamboos lush, flowers blooming. Some old people are doing t'ai chi. Kids are flying their kites as their grandparents run after them.

The baby boy is now in the Wenzhou couple's arms. In turn, the wife and the husband thoroughly check him over, studying him like a pair of newly-made shoes. They turn him upside down, check his ears, eyes, teeth, nostrils, fingers, legs, toes, as well as his bottom and his penis. Oddly enough, the baby doesn't cry this time. He seems to enjoy this sudden attention, and he starts to giggle.

Finally, the Wenzhou woman is satisfied and asks the young couple: 'Do you have a name for him?'

'Not really. Just for the hospital registration, we called him Wei Yu – that's the combination of our family names,' Weiming answers.

'In that case we will give him a great name, the best name a man can bear!' The Wenzhou man says in an inspired voice.

They find a quiet area of the park, beside a lake surrounded by leafy willow trees. There, no one can see what's going on. The water is clear, red carp swimming on the bottom. Lotus plants grow densely and lush, dragonflies are skating on the surface of the water. The Wenzhou woman volunteers to stand guard and walks away from their little group. The Wenzhou man puts his suitcase on the ground and takes out the blue plastic bag. Grabbing a bundle of money, Weiming starts to count, carefully. From time to time, he also checks whether the notes are fake.

It takes too long; half the money is still uncounted. The Wenzhou man begins to look impatient, and Yuli gets restless too. She lays her baby on the ground, facing the lake, and starts counting another bundle of notes. After minutes of intense silence filled only with the flicking of the banknotes, they reach their conclusion: exactly sixteen thousand yuan, no cheating. Weiming starts to gather the money, when suddenly there's a scream.

'Where is my baby?' Yuli cries, panicked.

They look around them, but there is no baby, only a suitcase lying empty on the ground.

The Wenzhou woman is just returning. As she approaches, her face changes colour. All three follow her gaze towards the water. As their eyes settle on the glassy surface, they see a baby sinking silently toward the bottom of the clear, beautiful lake.

DEAD CAN DANCE

It all begins with a tube of toothpaste. He doesn't even know what brand of toothpaste it is.

It is daybreak and in a half-waking trance, his eyes open ever so slightly. It is as if he's in a test tube. The room is empty; there is not a sound. Gradually, the outside world seeps in, like water trickling through the walls. Old women are bickering out there and fruitsellers are passing by, and he doesn't need to open the curtains to know that the sun's shadow has reached the fifth panel in the fence. Or that the iron railings are covered with countless quilts baking in the sun and that some are being thwack-thwack-thwacked with wooden beaters. He rolls over to find that the girl lying next to him has her eyes open too, as if in deep contemplation.

'Put some music on, will you?' She sighs languidly.

'What do you fancy?' he asks as he sits up and lights a cigarette.

She strokes his slightly bulging belly. 'You look middle-aged.'

He exhales a puff of smoke and glances down at his midriff.

'You choose, put on whatever. I just need noise,' she says.

He gets up off the mattress. Naked save his glowing cigarette, he enters a plastic metropolis of towers constructed entirely from CD cases. He is engrossed and puts great thought into his selection. He wants to choose something a girl would like. He's beginning to like this girl lying on his bed.

His cigarette is smoked down to the butt before he finds something to his liking. He puts the CD in the stereo and the apartment fills with music. Weird music.

She smiles. '"Dead Can Dance", I like that name.'

He gets up and turns over the sofa cushions in search of his clothes. So far he has found a pair of trousers, which he has pulled on. He sits down in the wicker chair beneath the window and rests his feet on the table. He is smoking in deep gulps, like a parched traveller in the desert. He watches as the girl disappears into the bathroom, and pulls the curtain open just an inch.

On the windowsill sits a lily he bought two days ago. It is withered to the brink of death.

Dead Can Dance. Dead Can Dance.

The noise infuses the entire room. It sounds like music for a funeral.

It's 9.10 a.m. when he checks his watch. He can hear the jets of water ricocheting off the bathroom walls. A couple of minutes later she appears at the bedroom door, her sodden hair dripping. She's holding a toothbrush in one hand and her mouth is brimming with bubbles.

'I've used up the last little bit of your toothpaste,' she says casually, and then continues to brush.

He finishes his second cigarette of the morning and stubs the butt out in the ashtray. It's already full with last night's fag ends.

'I'll go to the supermarket next door and get some more.' He stands up to leave.

'I could go...' she says as she wanders into the bathroom.

The sound of running water stops. There is a tinny clatter as a toothbrush is dropped into a cup.

Then she's back in the bedroom, where she picks up a brush on the table in front of the mirror and begins to brush her long hair. A constant trickle of water falls to the floor. He can make out four or five strands of her hair mingled with the droplets by his feet.

She starts to dress, item by item. First a white singlet – she doesn't wear a bra underneath. As she slips the top over her head her gaze sweeps over the bed. Her eyes are cold, void almost, as she bends down towards the floor in search of a pair of white tights. She finds them and then slides on a blue skirt with a slit up the back. She is skinny, with a childlike body.

'Do you have any change?' she asks.

He gives her a five-yuan note. She plucks the note from his hand and walks towards the door, stopping to put on a pair of sandals with precariously thin straps. He opens the door for her and says: 'I'll put the kettle on. Once you're back with the toothpaste, we'll have some coffee.'

She does not respond, walking straight out the door, her wet hair wagging against her exposed shoulders.

After closing the door he notices the girl's rucksack still hanging from the back of a chair. So she wasn't leaving. Of course, she's just gone to buy toothpaste.

The sound of her sandals slapping on the concrete hallway fades as she heads down the corridor. His mind is full of her moist hair and how the dampness will evaporate in the few moments she is outside under the glare of the sun. He walks to the kitchen, fills the kettle under the tap, lights the gas stove and starts to boil some water.

Then he wanders through to the bathroom where, sure enough, the tubes of toothpaste, two of Crest and a local brand, all caps off, are shrunken and empty. He tosses them in the bin.

He begins spreading shaving foam over his chin and moments later his face is covered in lather.

Unlike the previous times they had met, last night she had been the one to approach him, she made the first move, but now she seems distant and withdrawn. It pains him. And at that moment he decides he needs to make an effort to keep this girl – by shaving, maybe, or somehow preparing for life as a couple, as two people joined together. A life that could begin with a new tube of toothpaste.

He moves to the small shaving mirror and picks up his razor, then, slowly, begins to shave. The first strokes are from his left ear to cheek, then from the bottom of his neck to the jawbone.

By the time I've finished shaving, he thinks to himself, she will be back from buying the toothpaste.

The sound of high heels comes from the corridor outside, sharp and rhythmic high heels, thin and slender high heels. That's not his girl. He carries on shaving, but a hint of anxiety slowly sneaks into his mind.

Dead Can Dance. The bedroom brims with the melody's drumbeats, groans and wails. It has the sound of tribal music.

His mind wanders for a moment and in that second of broken thoughts a crack of blood emerges from the skin by his mouth. He pulls the razor away; with a look of shock on his face he examines himself in the mirror. He raises a finger to the cut and touches it softly, not knowing what to do.

He rinses the razor under the running water then dabs the wound with a hand towel. He isn't feeling quite right.

The walkway is silent now, and he knows she should be back from the supermarket. Maybe she's leaving the checkout at this very moment, and now she's sauntering through the entrance, or maybe she's stopped off at the florist's to buy some flowers. The lily on the windowsill is withered and women notice that kind of thing.

He raises a hand and touches the stripe of crusty scab from an old cut in the hollow of his cheek, as the kettle's piercing whistle grows louder. He walks into the kitchen and turns down the gas. She should definitely be back by the time this tiny flame has boiled the water again, he decides.

Back in the bathroom he turns to the other side of his face and starts shaving off the rest of his stubble with deliberate clean strokes. As he shaves he has an expression of complete concentration, absorbed in the task.

He is now clean-shaven and has washed his face. He turns off the tap.

He walks from the bathroom through to the living room and stares at her black rucksack hanging behind the chair. It occurs to him then that she has worn this same black bag each time they've met, yet he knows nothing of its contents. With that thought he returns to the bedroom. The CD is still playing, the funeral procession still singing.

He is beginning to run out of ways to busy himself. His mood is starting to alter, ever so gradually.

His throat feels raw and tickly. He flings open the curtain with intent. The sun's intense light dazzles him and he instinctively draws it back. As he drops his hand it brushes past the sickly lily and a handful of wilted petals flutter to the floor.

He sits down on the mattress, lighting another cigarette, an attempt to relieve his growing anxiety.

It's his third cigarette of the morning.

It's his third cigarette before brushing his teeth.

When his third cigarette is smoked down to the butt he gets up off the bed and stands. He is utterly lost now and begins to pace, up and down, between the kitchen and the bedroom. Eventually he picks up two cups and spoons a helping of instant coffee into each one.

And then he sits down on the mattress, again.

The heavy footsteps of a man wearing chunky boots reach him from the corridor outside, then the hushed tread of old people's cotton slip-ons and the swift passing of a running child – then cries and sniffles as he tumbles over. But there isn't the sound of plastic sandals striding along concrete. That pair of plastic sandals, each held on by two precariously thin straps.

The ashtray is now an overfed and oversized mound of singed paper. He gets up off the mattress and tips its contents into the bin. It is empty only momentarily before it is filled with a new pile of glowing butts.

Tick, tock, tick, tock goes the clock hanging on the wall and the incessant march of the mechanical hands infuriates him.

In his frustration he realises – in a moment of clarity – that he likes this girl; or perhaps, even, that he has decided to love this girl.

He is in agony while he awaits her return. Or perhaps it is the effect of his wait that is a growing agony. It's the kind of suffering that breeds and multiplies with each passing second. It's not unlike being shot at, being shot at time and again, in a long-drawn-out gunfight. Not just mental anguish, but physical injury too.

He sits back down on the bed and smokes. Despair. Cavernous, consuming despair. Waiting, expecting her to return, waiting for her to appear, the yearning devours him. The sense of overpowering desire, of bottomless yearning, only drives him deeper into the darkness.

The water is boiling and the kettle is screeching. Louder

and louder it calls to him, but he does not hear it. He has forgotten the kettle; it is just an object for him, like all the motionless furniture surrounding him. It continues to cry in wretched shrill screams and before long the kitchen is shrouded in a haze of wispy mist, like a volcano before it erupts.

Time passes, it could be fourteen or fifteen minutes, it could be half an hour, or an hour, even two hours, but for him, it seems an entire century has slipped by. In just one morning he has grown old waiting. He has aged beyond recognition.

And eventually, time stands perfectly still while he sits there in an empty flat, losing himself.

The kettle's calls loses pitch and volume and fades until it is almost silent. He is oblivious to it all. He knows that the generous scoops of instant coffee in the cups on the kitchen counter are still dry. Not one cup, but two.

The stereo must be on repeat, the same CD continues to play, track after track until the disc finishes, and then starts over again.

Dead Can Dance. Dead Can Dance.

Suffering oozes down through the ceiling, every last drop seeping through every inch of his skin. Waiting for a lover who will not return is to undergo an exquisite pain. It suffocates him.

He isn't smoking any more. The whites of his eyes are red and he coughs.

With that cough he knows that his girl is never coming back. She has vanished.

★

The kettle in the kitchen has screamed itself hoarse. It waits silently on the gas stove. In the smoke.

Smoke, like his suffering, is all-consuming and envelops every object in the apartment. It permeates the space between his bones. This fastidious smoke, with meticulous attention to detail, even wraps itself around the empty tubes of toothpaste discarded in the bathroom bin.

BEIJING MORNING STAR

Beijing Morning Star
Current Affairs, pages 1–3
14 07 2008

Due to accusations and criticism from the United Nations concerning China's human rights record, China's People's Court has decided on a reform of the way the death penalty will be administered. From now on the method will be lethal injection rather than gunshot. The officials explained that this measure had been introduced to make the process more humane.

8.45 a.m., and Chief Editor Zhang had only just arrived at his office. It was July; he was sweating through his freshly-ironed white shirt. With his half-eaten breakfast in his hand and food collecting in his beard, the Chief did not look very respectable. He turned on the air conditioning, made himself a cup of green tea, sat down and started to check the articles for the next day's edition. The phrase '*lethal injection*' made him feel slightly uneasy. His eyes went back and forth along the line: '*The officials explained that this measure had been introduced to make the process more humane.*' He sipped his tea, swallowed the last bite of his pork and mushroom steamed bun, and called journalist Yu to his desk.

After a brief discussion with Yu, Chief Editor Zhang rewrote the article as follows:

```
The People's government has been
collecting opinions from the public
about the death penalty. As a result,
the People's Court has decided on a
significant reform about the way death
sentences will be administered. From
now on the method will be lethal injec-
tion rather than gunshot. The lethal
injection allows for a peaceful and
painless death, and it is fast as well
as economical. This method will there-
fore help improve the human rights
record of the country.
```

Journalist Yu was happy with the revision, although he wasn't convinced that lethal injections were indeed cheaper than bullets. But he assumed that the cost issues weren't important. He went back to his desk and continued working on other articles. After a few phone calls, he typed a news tagline, and showed it to his editor-in-chief:

Beijing Morning Star
Eating Out, page 10

14 07 2008

```
KFC    restaurants    in    Beijing    have
announced that they will stop selling
Sky-green soup, as the Health Control
Bureau  found  cadmium  in  it,  an  ex-
tremely  poisonous  element  which  can
cause cancer. This means that the only
Chinese dish sold by this Western chain
will no longer be available.
```

Chief Editor Zhang was reading Yu's article carefully. He knew this Sky-green soup very well – he often ate it with his wife and his ten-year-old son. Now he was surprised to learn this bad news, but even more surprised that his journalist had reported it. Fearful that KFC might sue his newspaper, he immediately altered Yu's text.

```
KFC restaurants have become extremely
popular  in  Beijing,  especially  with
children. They now count as key family
```

dining spaces. Their Sky-green soup is
one of the few Chinese dishes they
serve, and is a great favourite with
all their customers. Unfortunately,
KFC have today announced that they are
going to stop selling the soup, as some
unfriendly chemicals have been found in
it that might cause disease. Apart from
that, all the hamburgers, sandwiches
and French fries have been found to
be healthy for everyone to eat and
enjoy.

There was not much time left before the deadline for
tomorrow's publication, so Yu was in a hurry typing the
corrections on his computer.

Then Zhang read and checked articles by some of the
newspaper's other journalists:

Beijing Morning Star
Current Affairs, pages 1–3
14 07 2008

On Monday morning, pupils from ele-
mentary schools in Beijing took part
in the 'Green Olympics' programme aimed
at promoting water conservation. This
session was to promote the slogan 'Save
a bucket of water, let the flowers of

```
the Olympics bloom'. Mass dance forma-
tions representing drops of water and
flowers were performed. Large numbers
attended.
```

This was certainly a piece of good and joyful news. The
Editor-in-Chief approved it, and instructed the layout designer
to put it on the front page, beside another article:

```
In the Olympics crisis, China today
expressed its indignation and opposi-
tion to a resolution on Tibet adopted
by the US Senate. According to our
Foreign Ministry spokeswoman, Jiang
Yu, this resolution 'persistently
favours the Dalai clique and interferes
with China's internal affairs'. Jiang
urged the US to see through the Dalai
Lama's true motives, which she said
were to engage in secessionist activi-
ties under the guise of religion.
```

Zhang checked each word, and pondered on the article for a
good while. Yes, it was a sensitive news story, he admitted. But
the article was written from China's point of view and made
the government's anti-US position clear. So there should be
no problem. The Editor-in-Chief made up his mind and
approved the text.

Zhang made himself another cup of tea, then went out onto the balcony to smoke. He looked at the concrete horizon, brand-new shiny buildings shimmering in the summer-morning sun; everything in this city seemed so well organised, the highways, the streets, the car parks, even the patches of grass seemed cut straight from a map. He felt he was living among a rigid army, but there was no chance for any war to be waged. What a thought, a war! he murmured to himself. Then he remembered that Chairman Mao had said that wars are necessary sometimes. He looked at his watch, collected his thoughts, stepped on his finished cigarette and went back inside.

Wang, a young female journalist who was in charge of the page 4 column 'Everyday Knowledge', was waiting at Zhang's desk, ready to show him a short piece:

Beijing Morning Star
Everyday Knowledge, page 4
14 07 08

Who invented football? The UK or China? Chinese historians agree that it was undoubtedly originally invented in China during the Chunqiu Dynasty, 3,000 years ago. It was called cu ju, and was played by eunuchs at the back of the emperor's palace. Nowadays, the game has become global. In 2002, the People's Republic of China's national football team qualified for the first time ever for the World Cup, thus putting our football playing back on the world map.

Chief Editor Zhang was happy with the little article, plus, he was always much more relaxed about the entertainment pages in the paper, where he knew it was not as easy to make a political mistake as in the news columns. Nevertheless, he readjusted a few words just to make the story a bit more interesting:

Everybody knows that football is the world's most popular game. But do you know it was originally invented in China, during the Chunqiu Dynasty? It was called cu ju. Thus, contrary to common belief, football was not invented in the UK. In 2002, the People's Republic of China's national football team honourably qualified for the World Cup. So the country that invented the game can once again finally compete among the world's strongest teams. It is becoming clear that Chinese football has a great future and that our country will very soon become the world's leading team.

At that point, Jiang, a very experienced journalist who had been with the paper for a while, who was in charge of the consumer section on pages 5 and 6, emailed Chief Editor Zhang some facts.

Beijing Morning Star
Business and Retail, page 6

14 07 08

It has been estimated that the consumption of moon cakes has this year risen to twice the level of last year. Although the government is checking on the high prices demanded by some independent private cake sellers, they have found that since last week early subscriptions from government work units and schools are increasing day by day. The People's Consumption Monitoring Bureau says that the total turnover for moon cakes this year will reach 100 billion yuan. And it is believed that places like Taiwan, Malaysia and the Philippines will start ordering cakes from China too. Thus the moon cake, one of the famous products from the ancient Chinese moon festival celebration, is gaining increasing popularity and promotion around the world.

Zhang smiled at the article – this was fine news, the only wording he needed to change was from '*places like Taiwan*' into '*provinces like Taiwan*'. Apart from that, he was happy with the piece. He liked this kind of news: selling moon cakes, how to keep your hair dandruff-free, how to grow a cactus or how to make the washing machine save water – the more insignificant, the better. And meanwhile, he reminded himself that he must order some moon cakes for his employers, and also some to take home for his family. It was a politically correct and friendly present, better than giving people cigarettes or alcohol. Now, as he made himself his third cup of tea, and as he reached the last section of the paper to check – the Advertisement Column – he received a phone call from the Beijing Media Censorship Bureau. The man on the phone spoke in a clear and mechanical voice, as if it was a pre-recorded answer machine.

'Hello, Editor-in-Chief, we are calling to officially inform you that your newspaper will be closed from today until further notice, due to an article published three months ago. You are requested to come to the Censorship Bureau Office at 2 p.m. today for self-criticism and a detailed report.'

Due to an article pubished three months ago? Zhang murmured to himself. Which one? He racked his mind for anything political or anti-public opinion, but with the telephone shaking in his hand he came to the conclusion that everything could be political or anti-public opinion from a censorship point of view. Daring not to ask for any specifics, he soberly answered: 'Yes, I will be there at 2 p.m.'

Chief Editor Zhang hung up the phone. He was paralysed on his chair for a few seconds, then he slowly drank the rest of his tea. He stood up, he tried to be as calm as possible; he said nothing to his staff. He picked up his briefcase, walked through the office, got into the lift and, stepping out onto the street, started to walk under the gradually heated Beijing morning sun.

INTO THE WORLD

Yujun

Walking in a daze, I was captivated by a cloud speeding across the sky. My eyes blurred, my hair nearly burnt by the summer sun. I imagined myself becoming Nazha – the young god from mythical fables with many arms. I saw myself like him flying through the sky riding on a wheel of fire under each foot. Yeah, I could see myself as Nazha in this boiling hot big city. This sharp weather shocks my body – Beijing is so unlike home. I have been here six months now and the heat still pricks me. I am used to days and days of rain in my village. My friends and I munch on chillies and garlic to keep us strong; they are still sitting at home waiting for the rain to stop, while chewing on local chilli beef. And I am here in Beijing: the capital, the government buildings, the city gate, the international corporations, the grand shopping centre.

The crowds and the traffic make me hazy and restless.

I remember it took me half a day to find the scriptwriter's house on that first morning. Big Beijing is a many-tunnelled maze and I couldn't find my way. He lives on a brand-new suburban estate – Gathering Dragon Garden. I couldn't believe it! – There were many guards working on the gate, and others wandering around the residential gardens in their uniforms. They spoke dialect, like me, and seemed to be doing little but making sure peasants didn't linger by the gate. Now I walk past them every day and we nod at each other.

I was so hot, and I sweated so much into my shirt that I felt smelly and drained. But I was immediately impressed by the scriptwriter. I felt he would teach me a lot about life. He is in his forties, I think. He wears a pair of thick glasses just like one of my old teachers at school. He's thin and bony and his hair is closely sheared like a monk's. Most of the time he sits at home, wrapped in his luxurious white robe, smoking non-stop and thinking hard. That first day I didn't see anyone else, just the scriptwriter. No family, no wife, no children.

Ning

It's so strange having someone around me every hour of every day. I have always lived alone. No cat, no dog, no living being has ever managed to survive under my roof. There was once a potted palm tree given to me as a New Year's gift by a film-maker I knew vaguely; still, even that lasted only a few days.

I have no need for a cleaner in my house – I like my

solitude, I am accustomed to it. But a very important cine-matographer insisted I should hire a cheap labourer he knew. 'You will be so glad to have him,' he said, 'it's like having three or four arms.' And I thought, but did not say: I only need one arm to write. But I finally acquiesced, much to his delight, and he added that his young peasant was very useful. Useful: that is supposed to be the most important quality for a man in this world.

Yujun

My first day in Beijing – madness! I felt like a young fawn in the wood – the lights, colours, noises were like rustles in the undergrowth making me dart here and there. It was too much! I remember I ran all over the city like a whirlwind. Everywhere the huge Olympics posters on the walls and everywhere the houses rising taller and taller. I wanted to see it all. But I also needed a job, I needed to be useful.

I got so lost, I remember. Then I found myself under a large sign saying Three Treasure Film Studios. As the traffic lights changed, a flood of young men rushed across the road and into the studios. They were hassling a bearded man dressed in a long black coat holding a clipboard and looking like some powerful agent. He was choosing people from the crowd, and suddenly he turned to me.

'Are you looking for work?' And then, 'Come with me.' I hesitated. 'Come on, boy! There's plenty here will have this job if you don't!'

'But where to?' I could hear my voice sounding nervous and high. One of the other men answered me. 'To move props for a film – we get fifty yuan and two meals a day.' Luck has fallen on my head, I thought, and today I am a lucky man.

Ning

The young peasant Yujun was three hours late the first day he came to see me. He spluttered and apologised and stood awkwardly in my hallway, so shy he didn't know where to put his feet and hands. He was wearing an orange T-shirt, as if borrowed from a university student; his blue jeans hung loose on his boyish hips, and the lace of his left trainer was untied and trailing along the floor. I nearly told him to do it up.

As we walked around the flat he stared, bewildered, at my grand writing table, his lovely face utterly confused. It made me smile, but I said nothing. I don't think he understood my job at all. He started to sneeze – perhaps the old books and the dust didn't suit him? My house is littered with rotten manuscripts and half-drunk bottles of gin, and it reeks of that intoxicating mix of musty paper and tobacco tang. I just love that smell.

Initially I gave Yujun only menial tasks. He cooked and swept and wiped and washed and scrubbed. At first I was worried he would dislodge my many piles of half-finished drafts of scripts and muddle them up, or clear my stacks of old papers into the dustbin. And for those first few days we spoke very little; I liked it like that – there was nothing to be said, as far as I was concerned. But then when he started to call me Script Master, I felt uneasy.

'Don't call me Script Master,' I would tell him, sighing, 'really I am quite pathetic.'

'Pathetic?'

Yujun seemed baffled, and smiled childishly. 'But how can someone who has written all those stories be called pathetic?' I had no answer for him.

Yujun

That first day Script Master gave me a brief tour of his house. He was quiet – so quiet! I felt like my footsteps were a giant's feet tramping around after him. He showed me the large living room where he spent most of his time. The sun shone so brightly that day and in between the curtains I could see thousands of specks of dust in the air. And there were so many books! I had never seen so many books. It's like living in the National Library! The four walls were completely covered by bookshelves. I also spied an antique typewriter tucked away in a corner: I looked at it in admiration, trying not to inhale the thick dust on its surface. In the centre of the room was a table so gigantic it took up half the space.

I felt uncomfortable circling the grand table in the middle of the room. Back then it almost scared me – it was so imposing, like the emperor's golden throne. On the table sat a silver laptop with a stack of beige machines behind it: printer, scanner, telephone and fax machine. Tall piles of bound manuscripts were scattered all over the table – I strained to read the titles: *Death by Radiation, The Garden of a Dunce, My Life as a Light Bulb Salesman, A Modern Romance – Love of Money, Sensations in Criminal Investigation*, and *Trust Me, I'm a Policeman*. And each was numbered: Draft 3, Draft 4, Draft 5 and so on. I wanted to read them all, but I was there to work, I was there to clean his windows, mop his floor and empty his rubbish bin. I knew my place; I was just a young peasant. I didn't have the time or the nerve to sprawl on the sofa and read. Anyway, I wasn't sure I could understand the ideas he wrote about.

This was a totally different world compared with my last job on the filmset: here was a place of silence. The Script Master seemed to dislike speaking, but his face was so expressive that I got to know him just by watching. I started to recognise his behaviour and habits: I knew that when the skin between his eyebrows sagged he was not to be disturbed; when his cigarette didn't leave his fingers, he didn't want to eat. His concentration was amazing – I could hardly believe that one man alone could write so many words! Definitely something my thick thumbs couldn't do. I started calling Ning 'the Script Master' after a few days and the name stuck.

Ning

I observe this stranger: always wearing his worn loose blue jeans and always smiling. I wonder if he has a childhood sweetheart in his home town. Perhaps he is even engaged to a village girl. Perhaps she is waiting for him to return one day, or maybe his heart will swell in this huge smoky city, and he will never want to return. All that's waiting for him at home is a plate of tofu and hard farm work. He seems a happy and simple boy, but I wonder if one day he will grow as old, grey and disillusioned as me.

Yujun

In Ning's house every object seemed to hide a secret from me. The first time I opened the curtains the Script Master's throat crackled oddly – I didn't know what I had done wrong. But I remember looking round in astonishment; ever since then I have kept the curtains drawn.

Even now after I've worked for him for a few months, I still study the master's behaviour: I notice how he winces at the slightest noise, like the flush of the toilet downstairs, the sizzle from a neighbour's wok, or the chatter of the bored guards outside the window. All these sounds distract him from his thoughts. Some days I wish I could grow wings and float silently around the house. And on other days I wish he would notice me or we could sit and drink tea and smoke his Camels together, or he would finally talk to me.

Ning

One morning I broke the eternal silence that exists between Yujun and myself and started talking to him. He looked surprised, but pleased, I think. I said: 'When I was your age, I read a lot,' and, 'I studied away from home and then came to the city to work.' On our first day Yujun had told me that he comes from a small village in the mountains where his family make tons of tofu to sell at the local market; he told me about their feet crushing the soya beans on the bare ground, the juice from the beans seeping out and running in little streams. I can barely imagine what that must be like. We are so different; there are chasms in our silence.

Yujun

I respect the Script Master's lifestyle: most nights I stay until he goes to bed, then I tidy the living room. Every second meal, I cook spicy Sichuan cuisine with lots of red chillies – my home town style. And my master seems to really enjoy it! I have started to feel that the Script Master's home is mine too. Sometimes, I pick a book from the shelf and read. I remember once I chose a book called *The History of Sexuality* written by some foreigner, but I couldn't understand a single thing. There was a photo of the author on the cover – he wears a leather jacket and thick black glasses but has no hair. Another time, I selected a book called *Emperors: The Unofficial Story*. What I read stunned me: I would never have thought that our revered emperors would do such things with boys.

Has my head got hazy and my brain grown bigger since my arrival at the Script Master's house? I'm sure it has: I was born a peasant, and according to my family book, eighteen generations of my ancestors have been peasants. But now I feel like I could maybe change my fate by staying with this man and learning from him and his books.

It was the same every day from the moment I started working for the Script Master. But then one day my master talked to me properly for the first time. He spoke slowly and it almost seemed like he wasn't talking to anyone in particular. I didn't know what to say! He told me about his childhood   I had guessed that my master came from a city family and always wondered if he could imagine what life is like when you grow soya beans on a mountainside for a living, like my family have been doing all their life. As we talked it also seemed to me that my master's life was not real. He told me, 'I like to live in my mind.' For me the mind is not a real place, but I have always remembered that sentence.

Ning

Sitting on a chair, writing day and night, is like being in a coma. The body becomes imprisoned by thoughts, the outside world cannot enter. I have been in this coma ever since I decided to write. I used to have a pure vision of writing: once I only wrote poems, but the publishers turned them down and I never saw my poems in print. Then I started writing martial arts novels but I could never believe in them enough to get more than halfway through; and ever since I have written only for others. I have seen through the fantasy of love; I know now that love can only exist in stories. Although my body is aching for another person's warmth, my mind is clear and cold.

Yujun

About a month ago the Script Master came to talk to me while I was making his lunch. He lent me a green bicycle and asked me to deliver some manuscripts for him. From that day on I cycled a lot, carrying large volumes, picking up newspapers for him and seeing all of Beijing on my wheels – I am becoming Nazha. I even rode down to the bottom of the Great Wall.

Then one day last week everything changed. He talked for hours on the phone that day, seething with anger. I had never heard him speak so much or shout with such ferocity. I knew that my master was in trouble. From the kitchen, I could hear his chair thump down on the rug at the end of each sentence. It sounded like he was arguing about his script. I soon realised that the target of Ning's tirade was a producer. My master was cursing the producer, calling him an 'uncultured' man. He shouted down the phone. 'You're a piece of shit. We all know how you used to drive about in your "Get Rich" taxi. You know more about horseshit than you do about films – every script you touch turns to pig piss,' and so on. I was so shocked – I've never heard Script Master using such language before.

The argument seemed to carry on forever. I think it was about money, but I could only hear one side of the conversation. I felt furious for him. So angry that Script Master had spent every waking hour of a whole year writing this script and the producer hadn't given him a penny.

My master had been swindled.

I heard the telephone being thrown back on the table and the bursting sound of my master swearing. He began to pound noisily on the keyboard. I tiptoed down the corridor and glanced at him. His brow was furrowed and his face was ashen. Writing truly is harder than labouring as a blacksmith or toiling in a factory, I thought. As a blacksmith or a labourer, you can't be cheated too badly. In absolute silence, I began to sweep the carpet around him. While my master tried to immerse himself in work, his ghostly pale face gradually became streaked with scarlet.

The thumps from the keyboard slowed down until eventually I heard him stop writing altogether. He lit a cigarette, took a sip of cold tea and began to pace the length of the table. Suddenly he raised his fists in the air and shouted, 'No more!' I stared at him, and then I whispered, 'If I can be of service in any other way...'

'Nobody can help me with this!' His voice was hoarse. His hair drooped down and covered his eyes and I saw that his old, crumpled jumper was on the wrong way round. I almost wanted to lay my hand on his hand.

After a while, my master seemed to change his mind and I remember he looked at me with a helpless expression. 'Will you listen to my grumbling?' He sat down in his rattan chair and I curled up at his feet and listened.

'The first draft of this script took me fourteen months to

write, day and night,' he stuttered, 'and then I spent yet more time revising it according to the producer's opinions. Months and months. You know – you've seen me at it! But when I delivered the final version, the producer just said it was a rubbish script and he refused to pay. As far as I can see, the producer doesn't have the money to pay me anyway, nor does he even have any budget for the production. He is a liar and a cheat. He uses my script to go hunting for money from rich people, the moment he secures this money he'll buy a fancy car or spend it on an expensive holiday in Thailand with his mistress. I know his type, he won't use it to fund the project. That's what all the thieves in the film industry do here in China.'

'How much does he owe you, Script Master?' I asked.

'One hundred and fifty thousand yuan. And if I don't get that money, there's no point in your coming back to work next week because I won't be able to pay you.' He looked desperate.

Ning

Once again life has proved to me that man is forever untrustworthy. I have spent so much of these last years writing that script, and now nothing will come of it. I should never have stopped writing poetry just for myself. I am exhausted.

Yujun

I watched the Script Master sitting in his chair all night. The ashtray was overflowing, an empty whisky bottle by his side, as the grey morning light seeped through the curtains. I dared not disturb him. I cooked some dumpling soup, but he had no interest in eating.

The next morning the producer called again and my master went as mad as the first time. He smashed the phone across the room and it shattered against the bookcase. Then the house was silent again.

As I swept the broken telephone from the floor, he grappled with the child lock on a bottle of sleeping pills. I couldn't just sit by and watch. I was worried – so worried! So I took the bottle from him and placed one tablet in his open palm. I looked at this poor, ragged, man who had brought me into civilisation and luxury through his trust and kindness. Suddenly, I had an idea.

'Do you want me to rough him up a bit?' I asked.

The Script Master didn't respond. For a long while he sat there staring at the swirling screensaver on his laptop, as if in a trance, and then he turned to me.

'Rough him up how?'

And so we talked, and after hours of discussion a plan was decided on: he knew the producer was in business with a karaoke bar owner who made his money smuggling cocaine into China. I would go to the producer's and hide round the back where he parked at night. I'd wait for him to come

101

home then attack him with a hammer. I would tell him that if the Script Master didn't get his money the police would receive a tip-off about his criminal dealings. My reward was to be ten per cent of the money – that was what the Script Master proposed.

I found a hammer in one of my master's kitchen drawers, then left his house under the glow of moonlight.

Ning

After Yujun left, I started pacing up and down the living room. I was worn out and restless. I went to bed with a nervous fever. My mind was full of regret. I fidgeted uncontrollably and fought off constant nausea. I had written dozens of cops and robbers stories – I knew almost every type of crime and murder – but I had never actually broken the law. I began doubting whether Yujun could go through with the plan, and felt even more miserable than I had done earlier. What if Yujun were to break his leg or the hammer were smashed into his lovely face?

Yujun

Early this morning I rode the Script Master's green bike into Gathering Dragon Garden, carrying a bulky bag weighed down by the hammer. No one noticed me; the guards were still sleeping in their shed. I opened the Script Master's door. He was there at his writing table – exactly as I had left him the night before – smoking a cigarette and sitting still like a statue, staring at me with his bloodshot eyes. I took the hammer out of the bag and as I washed the blood off under the tap, the Script Master remained silent. He continued to stare at me as if I was some sort of alien invading his house. I told him everything had gone exactly as planned, and assured him that no one had died. 'I left him with only a few injuries,' I said, 'nothing serious.' It was an easy mission for me – I am a strong peasant and a hammer is always a good tool. I told the master that the producer's face had split like a blossoming flower.

Then I took the money out of my bag, and laid it on the master's table. Both of us remained silent. After a moment, the Script Master put out his cigarette, counted out thirty thousand yuan and gave the notes to me – twice as much as we had agreed. I had never earned so much money in my entire life. I sat on the sofa, and started to worry about what I should do with it. Suddenly it felt as though all this money was worth nothing.

My master looked miserable; he didn't speak at all but peeked at the outside world through the gap in his curtains, as if he had come to the last day of his life. It was nearly lunch-time. I opened the fridge and started to prepare Mala tofu for him as if it were any normal day.

'I don't need anyone to serve me now,' my master said.

I didn't understand what he meant.

Avoiding my eyes, the Script Master stared at the tofu and went on. 'I will call you if I need you again.'

I didn't know what to think or what to answer. Silently, I cooked the tofu, my last tofu for the Script Master.

Ning

Today Yujun left. I am alone again, after all these months of having a lovable young man around. The kitchen is lonesome, the fridge stinks and there is no one to cook me my meals. I can feel dust already starting to accumulate on my books and floor again. I have a boundless feeling of emptiness. I can't bear to stay in this gloomy house any longer. And so I have decided to leave. Tomorrow morning I will pack my suitcase and buy a one way ticket to Putuo Mountain.

Putuo is an island in the East China Sea. It is the place to find peace. I can imagine my life there easily: I will read the Buddhist sutras, watch the birds flying between the trees, and listen to the great waves of the sea rising up and down under the clouds. I think, probably, I will be a happier man.

Yujun

So with the money my master gave me I have now rented a small room in a cheap area of Beijing. I have found myself a table, and a chair. I have a plan: each day I will buy a copy of the *Beijing Evening News*, and read every single word of it. I will scribble. Already today I have started to write down things that have been swimming about in my mind for a long time from those first crazy hot days when I arrived in Beijing.

Perhaps one day I will buy myself a green bicycle and ride it into the centre of Beijing. Perhaps I will ride to the Three Treasure Film Studios and see crowds of young men from the provinces hanging around by the gate, hungry for job opportunities. And I will think of a story that began many years ago, about a scriptwriter, whose life started as a poor migrant from the provinces. Then I will ride the bicycle back home, and write down a title on a blank piece of paper: *Into the World*.

ADDRESS UNKNOWN

From: xiling@yahoo.co.uk
To: nigelthomas1975@hotmail.com
Sent: 10.07.2009 03:32
Subject: Beijing calling

My dearest you,

So here I am. The twelve-hour flight from London to Beijing has worn me out. When I arrived in my neighbourhood yesterday, I couldn't find the entrance to my apartment. Almost every old building has been demolished, my house now stands by the highway. It feels strange, after four years living in a run-down street of London, I'm now back in this brand-new world, like living in a pastless city in America. I can no longer find my old familiar foodstall, and the pear trees that grew in a nearby alleyway have gone.

My flat is up in the high thin air where the aeroplanes pass, casting shadows into my room. From my bedroom window I've been watching the courtyard of the restaurant next door. The chefs and waiters shout at each other in a southern dialect. Their faces are dark, sunburnt, as if they've just left their rice paddies back home. Last night I saw them plucking ducks' feathers and cutting off pigs' feet. The scene looked oily and bloody – I thought perhaps they were making my favourite pork dumplings. Remember in London I just wanted to eat Chinese food every day. You know how I always hated English food – the sad salads without any salt! One good thing about being back here, I suppose.

It will be hard to sleep tonight. It's strange without your body next to mine. And there's so much noise – the restaurant chefs scream twenty-four hours a day, the construction work on the highway carries on and on – more trucks bringing more cement, even after midnight. It feels like no one sleeps in Beijing...

I will write to you soon. Bye for now.
Take care and love,
Your Ling x

From: xiling@yahoo.co.uk
To: nigelthomas1975@hotmail.com
Sent: 18.07.2009 10:35
Subject: Beijing calling again

My dearest you,

How are things in London? Are you seeing your friends? Are you managing to swim every morning as you used to? I called you twice today but couldn't reach you. Are you still working nights? Is it rainy there? It's almost 40 degrees here. Cars and air conditioning produce even more heat in this dusty city. Beijing is crazy – it's like a forty-year-old man trying cocaine for the first time. Everything is booming, regenerating, but in a twisted way.

In the morning I see old people coming out of their apartments – I think they are happier here than in the west because they live with their families and spend time with their grandchildren.

If we live together forever in a council house in east London we will never have this kind of life. We will die lonely. And you will die first, because women live longer than men. Then I will die alone, in a silent and gloomy flat, with only the sound of the TV from the Bengali family next door. It's so scary when I think of our old age. Maybe we should move back to China, and live like these people – energetic, strong, laughing all day from early in the morning.

I hope you manage to find yourself a good, solid bicycle

from Brick Lane market. Write to me soon.

Love,
Your Ling x

From: xiling@yahoo.co.uk
To: nigelthomas1975@hotmail.com
Sent: 26.07.2009   20:45
Subject: Where are you?

Dearest,

I haven't had any emails from you. I have called you many times, but no one answers the phone.

Have you already moved out of your flat? Before I left England you promised that you would tell me when you moved. I don't understand what's happening with you.

Here in Beijing the temperature continually rises. In those air-conditioned restaurants everyone talks about VC – venture capital – I guess it's an American word. Apparently it's a new way to make lots of money.

I spend my days wandering around in the busy streets; I can't decide if I like this country or not. I want to hear from you, my dearest – where are you?

Kisses,
Your Ling xx

From: xiling@yahoo.co.uk
To: nigelthomas1975@hotmail.com
Sent: 10.08.2009   22:57
Subject: You've disappeared!

Dearest,

Today is 10 August. I've now been back in China for a month.
But still I have heard nothing from you. I used to think the
world was small, and London was not really very far from
Beijing. But I was wrong.

Everyone asks me what England looks like, whether Westerners
are all very rich, and if they have sex with each other without
getting married. I can't answer them any more. Maybe you
can?

I miss the walks we used to take late at night along Regent's
Canal and the morning wind in Haggerston Park. I miss those
arguments we always had in Tate Modern; the bright green
leaves of the horse chestnut trees outside your flat.

I miss you.
Your Ling x

From: xiling@yahoo.co.uk

To: nigelthomas1975@hotmail.com

Sent: 20.08.2009   09:20

Subject: Is this your answer?

Dear you – I feel truly sad as I write down these words.

I have dialled your number almost every day, but I never hear anything back. I have also tried calling your friends, but they couldn't tell me where you were. I think they do know, but they don't want me to find out. People don't say straight things in the West. That's what I hate about it.

Here, I'm trying to live each day more or less like other people – buying vegetables, cooking meat, wandering around the cheap markets, watching pirate DVDs in the evening, thinking about family life and all that.

I'm sure you have received my emails, and I wonder if you'll ever write to me or call me.

I thought you might like to know that my father is not well. It's really, really hard. He doesn't recognise family members any more. I think he's dying – he needs me. So this morning I cancelled my flight. I won't be coming back to England this week.

I don't know when I will be in London again, maybe the day you write back to me, or maybe I will never return to England. But I know tonight I will think about that world on my pillow.

Take care, and still, love to you.

Your Ling x

THE THIRD TREE

Friday:

SENDER: J
+7771783477
17-07-2009 16:20
Hi, this is J, we met in the park
today, by the third tree near the
gate. Do you remember me?

SENDER: E
+7891533432
17-07-2009 16:23
Hello. Yes, I remember.

SENDER: J

+7771783477

17-07-2009 16:25

Never seen anyone sitting by that
tree, yet I walk past it everyday –
it's a perfect reading spot!

SENDER: E

+7891533432

17-07-2009 16:28

Thats odd because I reading by
that tree a lot now. Spring and
now summer, but summer in this
country is brief.

SENDER: J

+7771783477

17-07-2009 16:31

Hmm. Yes, summer here is brief.
Odd question – do you play
badminton? Game tomorrow at
London Fields? 4pm?

SENDER: E

+7891533432

17-07-2009 16:35

Sound good. Or maybe we play
table tennis?

SENDER: J

+7771783477

17-07-2009 16:37

Good Idea! I'm a pretty mean
player though.

SENDER: E

+7891533432

17-07-2009 16:41

No you cant be better than me. I
am an Asia. We are good at that.

SENDER: J

+7771783477

17-07-2009 16:45

I bet you're very good but you're
talking to a champion here. I won
youth championships at home in
New Zealand.

SENDER: E

+7891533432

17-07-2009 16:48

You from New Zealand! If you so
good I dont play with you. Sorry.

SENDER: J
+7771783477
17-07-09 16:52
Oh no – only joking! Actually I'm
totally hopeless at table tennis!
Do play. Please.

Saturday:

SENDER: E
+7891533432
18-07-2009 11:04
So sorry but I cant table tennis
today. Have to work late.

SENDER: J
+7771783477
10-07-2009 11:07
Pity. Bad for your health working
so late. What are you doing
tonight? Fancy getting a bite to
eat? Japanese? Maybe even
octopus sashimi?

SENDER: E
+7891533432
18-07-2009 11:10
Ah how you know exactly what
i want?

SENDER: J
+7771783477
18-07-2009 11:13
Maybe I have a little Japanese
in me.

SENDER: E
+7891533432
18-07-2009 11:16
Ok if eat Japanese then I say
place. Hiroshima, 6 Mare St, 7.

SENDER: J
+7771783477
18-07-2009 11:19
7? Are you sure – I thought you
said you had to work late...

SENDER: E
+7891533432
18-07-2009 11:22
I change my mind.

★ ★ ★

SENDER: J
+7771783477
18-09-2009 23:48
Thanks for a really lovely evening.
And such great sashimi too!

SENDER: E
+7891533432
18-07-2009 23:52
Not best octopus I've had. I prefer
walk we did through park after.

SENDER: J
+7771783477
18-07-2009 23:54
You smelt gently of saki.

SENDER: E
+7891533432
18-07-2009 23:57
Oh Im sorry.

SENDER: J
+777170J477
19-07-2009 00:01
No, I liked it very much. Sweet
dreams.

★ ★ ★

SENDER: J
+7771783477
19-07-2009 01:15
You asleep yet? You know I really
wanted to kiss you in the park.
There were shadows on your face
from the trees. I could smell your
beautiful black hair. Wish I had.

SENDER: E
+7891533432
19-07-2009 01:18
I have been breathing you since
we met. Your spirit wrapped
around me like smoke. Goodnight.

SENDER: J
+7771783477
19-07-2009 01:40
I've been lying awake thinking
about you. Why did you leave so
urgently in the park earlier?

Sunday:

SENDER: J
+7771783477
19-07-2009 09:30
Morning! Did you get my text last
night? Love to meet up today if
you've time. Same place by the
tree in the park? Hope you aren't
suffering too much from that
allergy.

SENDER: E
+7891533432
19-07-2009 09:36
Allergy is bad – trees in the park
make me sneeze too much. Maybe
we can meet later...I dont know.
What you doing today?

SENDER: J
+7771783477
19-07-2009 09:40
I might play my guitar, but should
really go to the library. Giving a
paper at a conference tomorrow
and need to work. Text me
whenever and I can meet you in
London Fields.

SENDER: E

+7891533432

19-07-2009 09:45

You play guitar? You write songs
too?

SENDER: J

+7771783477

19-07-2009 09:49

Yes – bad ones though! I actually
once wrote a song called 'The
Third Tree'.

SENDER: E

+7891533432

19-07-2009 09:51

The Third Tree! I can't believe it.
Hmm. Like our tree in park. What's
about?

SENDER: J

+7771783477

19-07-2009 09:52

It's about an apple tree in our
garden in NZ. About my childhood.
So, when can I see you?

SENDER: E
+7891533432
19-07-2009 09:55
Actually i dont think that good
idea. We should not have met.

SENDER: J
+7771783477
19-07-2009 09:58
I don't understand. What do
you mean?

SENDER: E
+7891533432
19-07-2009 10:03
Too complicated.

SENDER: J
+7771783477
19-07-2009 10:10
Ah, but I am a scientist. I am
particularly interested in
complicated subjects and you
are a perfect test specimen!

SENDER: E
+7891533432
19-07-2009 10:13
Anyway we shouldnt get
too close.

★ ★ ★

SENDER: J
+7771783477
19-07-2009 12:14
Hi! Come and have lunch with me?
And why shouldn't we get too
close? You are so lovely – I want to
know everything about you.

SENDER: E
+7891533432
19-07-2009 12:17
You dont have to know every
lovely thing.

SENDER: J
+7771783477
19-07-2009 12:21
But you are special. When I saw
you under the tree I knew you
were someone special, someone I
had to meet. Do the Japanese
believe in fate or destiny?

SENDER: E
+7891533432
19-07-2009 12:24
Yes. I believe in fate.

SENDER: J
+7771783477
19-07-2009 14:36
Hello again. All ok? Working hard?
Maybe you need a walk. Where
are you working?

SENDER: E
+7891533432
19-07-2009 14:40
I am in cafe reading. Same cafe
we ate last night. But not sure how
long i will stay here my nose cant
stop running.

SENDER: J
+7771783477
19-07-2009 14:45
Hold onto your nose   I've a
special kissing medicine that
works wonders! On my bike – be
there in 15 mins.

★ ★ ★

SENDER: J
+7771783477
19-07-2009 22:26
I miss your hair, your fingers. I
miss your smell. We live so close
to each other – why don't you
cross the park and come to
see me?

SENDER: E
+7891533432
19-07-2009 22:30
I miss you too...

SENDER: E
+7891533432
19-07-2009 22:34
Sorry i cannot.

* * *

SENDER: E
+7891533432
19-07-2009 23:01
So what you wear for tomorrow
conference speech?

124

SENDER: J

+7771783477

19-07-09 23:08

Good question! Well, I want to
promote a kind of artist/scientist
image.

SENDER: E

+7891533432

19-07-2009 23:14

How does that work? Science is
not art. You have to be precise
I thought.

SENDER: J

+7771783477

19-07-2009 23:19

True, but in my work I'm getting
closer to a version of your eastern
philosophy. Might not sound like
science but ultimately everything
leads to a state where the truth is.
I study how the brain perceives
these ideas.

SENDER: E

+7891533432

19-07-2009 23:22

Truth? I dont believe this word.
The truth of the world is there is
no truth.

SENDER: J

+7771783477

19-07-2009 23:24

Maybe you're right, in one sense.
But I'm still trying to prove the
impossible with science.

SENDER: E

+7891533432

19-07-2009 23:27

But you cant prove that. In japan
we believe zen: you cant know
world from your brain, you can
only know world by feeling it with
your heart.

SENDER: J

+7771783477

19-07-2009 23:31

Hmm, for me feeling is not the
final truth. Anyway, my love, can I
see you now?

SENDER: E

+7891533432

19-07-2009 23:33

No. It is a dangerous game.

SENDER: J

+7771783477

19-07-2009 23:37

Why dangerous? Are you saying
you're playing games with me?

SENDER: E

+7891533432

19-07-2009 23:42

No. I am fearful. Cant explain to
you in text message. I sigh.

SENDER: J

+7771783477

19-07-2009 23:46

Wish I could kiss your sad sighs
away. Am going for a late-night
stroll now. Come out and join me?

SENDER: E

+7891533432

19-07-2009 23:48

Sorry i cant come out now.

* * *

SENDER: J

+7771783477

20-07-2009 01:07

I think of you all the time. Can't
sleep. I want to see you now.

SENDER: E
+7891533432
20-07-2009 01:09
I can't sleep too. But we dont have
future.

SENDER: J
+7771783477
20-07-2009 01:12
You don't know what the future
holds. You can't decide the future
now. That's not fair.

Monday:

SENDER: E
+7891533432
20-07-2009 16:35
Hello. How was conference today?

SENDER: J
+7771783477
20-07-2009 16:37
It's actually not finished yet. Too
many scientists speaking about
neurones and hypotheses! They
drive me crazy, but they don't
distract me from thinking of you...

SENDER: E
+7891533432
20-07-2009 16:40
I cant work either. Today i miss
you badly.

SENDER: J
+7771783477
20-07-2009 16:43
Me too. Going to duck out of the
drinks here this evening – I will
run across London to see you.

SENDER: E
+7891533432
20-07-2009 16:47
I feel terrible, Incomplete. I feel
urge to see you. Like cherry
blossoms about to fall to the
ground in one night.

SENDER: J
+7771783477
20-07-2009 16:49
Meet me in front of my house at 7.
Can't wait to see you and kiss you.

Tuesday:

SENDER: E

+7891533432

21-07-2009 22:35

I start to paint again. This morning
i painted some images. They very
dark depressive. Dont know what
the shapes mean to me.

SENDER: J

+7771783477

21-07-2009 22:38

Sounds amazing! Would you show
me sometime? In fact, why do you
never invite me to your place?

SENDER: E

+7891533432

21-07-2009 22:41

Maybe one day i will. At least
show you the darkest painting i
have ever done.

SENDER: J

+7771783477

21-07-2009 22:44

I wonder what makes you paint
dark pictures.

SENDER: E

+7891533432

21-07-2009 22:49

Sometimes i feel very alone.
A kind of utter loneliness.

SENDER: J

+7771783477

21-07-2009 22:52

But I am with you. How can you
feel so lonely? I wish I could
embrace you right now.

Wednesday:

SENDER: J

+7771783477

22-07-2009 12:41

When can I see you today? I am
hungry for your touch.

SENDER: E

+7891533432

22-07-2009 12:43

Meet at cafe near bridge? They
have good lentil soup.

SENDER: J
+7771783477
22-07-2009 13:17
Where are you? I'm like a starfish
moving around without a brain.
I'm losing myself...

SENDER: E
+7891533432
22-07-2009 13:20
Im coming. I have problems with
HIM. But I leave now.

SENDER: J
+7771783477
22-07-2009 13:22
Him? Tell me everything when you
arrive. I want to hold you tight.

* * *

SENDER: J
+7771783477
22-07-2009 17:31
I watched you disappear down the
road. My body aching for you
again already. Your sweet scent.
Your silky skin. My body tingling
like a horse ready to jump. I want
to have you. I want your body to
belong to me always.

SENDER: E
+7891533432
22-07-2009 17:36
It was grey raining outside as i
walked home past canal. I just saw
huge fish swim through the water.
I have big decision on me now.

＊ ＊ ＊

SENDER: E
+7891533432
23-07-2009 00:12
It is like silent war here. Invisible
smoke in every corner of the
house. I am glad we talked today,
but im suffering. I cannot bear my
body separated from you. I am
sleeping here beside another
body and i am tormented.

SENDER: J
+7771783477
23-07-2009 00:15
Baby I want you so much. I wish
you were mine, not his. My
nervous system is going crazy at
the thought of you. Even my brain
doesn't function as before.

Thursday:

SENDER: J

+7771783477

23-07-2009 09:17

I'm still mesmerised by every
moment from yesterday. Woke up
with wonderful images of your
body filling my mind.

SENDER: E

+7891533432

23-07-2009 09:20

I wish my body is still with you.
I am aching. Want to be close to
you. I feel the deeper i attract to
you, the more painful my messy
situation. My life splits in two. The
life in this bed and the life in your
bed.

SENDER: J

+7771783477

23-07-2009 09:23

My body feels like it is swimming,
yet I want to be your protector
and provider. Like I am a hunter
bringing the catch back to his
woman. Laying it at your feet.

SENDER: E
+7891533432
23-07-2009 09:25
You mean like in ancient time, a
man comes home with deer meat
and wild fruit?

SENDER: J
+7771783477
23-07-2009 09:27
Exactly! And also something
beyond that as well. I want you to
be mine.

SENDER: E
+7891533432
23-07-2009 09:28
Please. Dont push me. What you
ask from me is impossibility.
I have built a place with HIM and i
have built my life around his
world. And you ask me to destroy
this.

SENDER: J
+7771783477
23-07-2009 09:31
Sorry, my darling, I just want to
see you and be with you always.
I cannot stand this situation.

SENDER: E
+7891533432
23-07-2009 09:34
Im not alone and i cant always lie.
I try and get out in little while. See
you by the third tree in 2 hour.

* * *

SENDER: J
+7771783477
23-07-2009 14:06
Sorry if I was too strong earlier. I
can't help it. I hope I didn't hurt
you. As I walked home through
London Fields I wished I was still
sucking you and drinking you and
entering you. I want you so much.

SENDER: E
+7891533432
23-07-2009 14:09
I feel burning. You came into me
too strong. You almost broke my
bones. I feel you are a bit
impulsive, when you pulling
my skirt.

SENDER: J
+7771783477
23-07-2009 14:11
I will kiss you better when I see you again. I am not impulsive – it just feels so beautiful to be with you, my darling.

SENDER: E
+7891533432
23-07-2009 14:14
But you makes me feel unsettled.

SENDER: J
+7771783477
23-07-2009 14:16
Maybe that's what love is – don't you think? I walk through the streets thinking: why aren't we together in a warm bed, embracing? I want nothing else.

SENDER: E
+7891533432
23-07-2009 14:19
You know why not. For scientist everything is possible to experiment, you kill something old for something new. You lose nothing in a lab.

SENDER: J
+7771783477
23-07-2009 14:21
But sometimes you only can
discover something new when old
things die.

SENDER: E
+7891533432
23-07-2009 14:25
Yes but love make me weak. I cant
do anything and i dont paint at all.
And i think i cant leave him for
someone I know only for few days.
Its madness.

SENDER: J
+7771783477
23-07-2009 14:28
No, my darling, it's not madness at
all! When I saw your face the
other day, I felt I had known you
for thousands of years.

★ ★ ★

SENDER: E

+7891533432

23-07-2009 19:45

I wish i cook for you like what I am
doing now for him. Cooking spicy
tofu with spinaches, boiling rice,
bare feet.

SENDER: J

+7771783477

23-07-2009 19:48

Hmmm that image of you is
strangely exciting. Maybe I will
cook us spicy tofu while you paint
with bare feet. Also I want to learn
Japanese. I want to know
everything!

* * *

SENDER: J

+7771783477

24-07-2009 02:28

Baby, are you awake? Are you ok?
I miss your texts. Just a small
syllable will do.

SENDER: E
+7891533432
24-07-2009 02:32
Yes, awake. We have been talking
all night. Oh god about loving two
people at the same time. It is
hard. But the conversation didnt
get far.

SENDER: J
+7771783477
24-07-2009 02:35
Are you really talking about
loving two people at once?

SENDER: E
+7891533432
24-07-2009 02:40
I want to find out how we can be
together, without hurting each
other. Also think if i move out
from his house, i dont move into
yours. Dont want to be someone's
woman again. I want to be a great
artist. I want to be like a monk.
To dedicate to my work.

Friday:

SENDER: J
+7771783477
24-07-2009 06:21
In this grey dawn I am filled with thoughts of you – and imagine sweet love between us. Come to me, my darling.

SENDER: E
+7891533432
24-07-2009 07:31
Sorry I just wake up. He's been upset and grey all night. I cried and cried. My eyes are sour and hair is entangled. My foot lose gravity. I need to be kissed and in your arms have a deep rest.

SENDER: J
+7771783477
24-07-2009 07:33
I'm here for you, my love.

★ ★ ★

SENDER: E
+7891533432
24-07-2009 20:40
I think i am not able to break
everything up to be with you.
Please forget about me.

SENDER: J
+7771783477
24-07-2009 20:42
What? Baby, where are you now?

SENDER: J
+7771783477
24-07-2009 20:44
Please speak to me.

SENDER: J
+7771783477
24-07-2009 21:03
Can you meet me by our tree?

SENDER: J
+7771783477
24-07-2009 21:05
Please, darling my love, please
answer me.

SENDER: J

+7771783477

24-07-2009 21:08

Darling darling, what's happened?
How can you make this decision
just like that? Can you see me?

SENDER: J

+7771783477

24-07-2009 21:12

Please, my love, I cannot believe
this is happening. Can you see me
now?

SENDER: J

+7771783477

24-07-2009 22:39

A blackness is coming over me. I
am going crazy.

SENDER: J

+7771783477

24-07-2009 22:41

I'm walking through the park in
the rain. It's so dark. I'm walking
past that tree, our tree. I'm
walking to your house. I have to
find you. Where are you?

SENDER: J
+7771783477
24-07-2009 22:43
Where are you?

SENDER: J
+7771783477
24-07-2009 22:45
Is it really over? For me it isn't.
You are throwing something very
special away – how can you do
this?

SENDER: J
+7771783477
24-07-2009 22:47
This can't be the end. Where are
you? Where are we? Can't you
answer the phone at least?

SENDER: J
+7771783477
24-07-2009 22:51
My love? Answer me!

ANYWHERE I LAY MY HEAD

7.49 a.m.

There's a small animal, very furry and white, called a three-toed sloth, that lives in the deep forests of the South American tropics. It is the sleepiest animal in the world, sometimes sleeping for twenty hours a day. It can live for up to thirty years and spend twenty years sleeping. I think I might be a sloth too, a five-toed sloth. Sleeping is what I need and love most.

'You sleep your life away,' Pierre always says. Pierre is my new boyfriend. I've only known him for a month, but I think Pierre has already guessed that I'm a five-toed sloth from China.

I can feel Pierre looking at me right now. Like a bird, he wakes up early, bright-eyed and alert. He is probably gazing at my misty forehead, waiting for me to wake up fully. He likes the way I sleep. Pierre says he feels a strong desire to love me when I am asleep, eyes closed, eyebrows quiet. He says I am beautiful when my big Chinese cheekbones don't move.

I know I sleep too much. Maybe it's because I am still young, though not that much younger than Pierre. I am twenty-five and he is twenty-eight, which may explain why I need three hours more sleep every day than he does. Pierre once watched a documentary about Chinese women workers, and his conclusion was that people in China never sleep. The women in the film worked day and night in factories making plastic bags and plastic toys, and when they weren't working they cooked huge bowls of noodles for themselves and their families, or ate them alone silently in makeshift restaurants or stared at the TV with blank tired eyes. I thought: I was studying so hard at home in China to get a scholarship for university here in the West – maybe I made myself so tired that now I need to catch up on all that sleep.

I have to wake up or I'll be late, I tell myself. In five seconds I have to open my eyes.

Raindrops obscure the view through the windows. The sky is grey, the clouds race past in a hurry. A September morning. It has been raining for a whole week, little drops falling on my coat, soaking my boots, every day, constantly. I hate it. Grey sky, grey garden, grey street, grey cafes and grey faces. Pierre hates English rain as much as I do. He says that French rain is better, at least French rain is more decisive and more romantic.

Pierre prefers the idea of living in Paris. Three years ago, when he left his little town near Avignon, he said he was taking a train to Paris. But I guess people rarely do what they intend to do and for some reason he only stayed in Paris for three days. He said his Parisian uncle got on his nerves, and it rained so much over those three days that he started to hate Paris; but I wonder whether someone also told him great things about London. Anyway, he jumped on a train at the Gare du Nord, crossed the Channel and arrived in England. It was an impulsive decision, he said, a decision without a reason, the decision itself was the reason. I like that, or maybe I like that kind of person. Because I am the same.

I decided to live with Pierre after only knowing him for three weeks. I like it that way. I like my skin beside another's skin. I like to feel their body temperature, even if I don't yet love that person.

8.49 a.m.

'I dreamt I was in my middle-school playground, and I wanted to do a somersault, and I failed. Everyone in the playground was looking at me, and some of the kids started to laugh. I tried again but my body was so heavy, like my grandmother's.' These are my first words today.

Pierre only listens; he has no comments, as if I am nothing but a radio by his pillow. I dream whenever I sleep, and then I tell Pierre what I can remember, as if he were Dr Freud. Perhaps he has already heard too many of my dreams, and it must be very boring for him. Recently some of my dreams have gone like this:

A. A maths exam in my high school. I couldn't divide 35 by 7, at which point my maths teacher turned into a giant King Kong and started to punish me with a whip.

B. An argument with an old communist about whether China is still a communist country – he cried out when he heard me saying that China is a capitalist country, and punched me hard on the nose.

C. A deserted high noon street with a river in the background – the river flows noiselessly like in a silent western movie.

D. A feast with the mayor of my home town in a very luxurious restaurant. We were served the biggest catfish I had ever seen – its whiskers were so long that we started using it as a skipping rope.

The strange thing is, though, I've been living in England for a few years now, but my dreams are still all set in China. In my dreams everyone is Chinese. It feels as if my life in the West amounts to nothing – there are no English faces, no Big Ben, no River Thames, no London Eye. The West is not there at all.

We kiss. Lips and eyes, eyes and lips. Then hair and ears, ears and hair. But I really need to get up – I have six hours of Chinese classes to teach. Troubled Westerners are waiting to be punished by a tough Chinese culture. I teach in a private language centre where the students are all older than me. They are bankers or businessmen wanting to open factories in China, so more Chinese peasant women can work day and night in their factories without wasting precious time sleeping.

Pierre turns on the radio. There's jazz playing, distorted. 'That's Chick Corea,' he says. Pierre is a musician, he recognises old tunes like this one. According to him, this piece is called 'Flight from Kaloof'. I listen for a few seconds and then start to wonder where Kaloof is. Kaloof sounds like Kowloon. Kowloon is in Hong Kong so perhaps Chick Corea has been flying from Hong Kong. I'm distracted by my thoughts as Pierre slides on top of me. The duvet slips onto the floor. Sunbeams burst through the window and strike our bodies. Pierre's lips are exploring my loins. The same familiar gentleness. But I wish there were thorns on his lips to wake me up.

My mobile phone rings. I lean across the bed to pick it up, and answer while Pierre is still kissing me.

'Hi, it's Laszlo.'

'Oh, hi.' I am a bit surprised. I shouldn't have taken this call.

Laszlo lives in Hungary most of the time, although he has a house in Notting Hill. I haven't heard from him for almost a year, and I don't know why he wants to speak to me now.

'Are you free today?' He asks in a hasty voice.

'No, not really.' I turn my body towards the bed. Pierre is looking at me searchingly. 'Why? Where are you?' I ask him in a detached voice. I know Laszlo; he will not give up easily.

'I arrive last night and I flying back to Budapest late late today. So I need to see you *now*.' His voice gets more pressing. I hold the phone to my ear but don't know what to say. 'Come here now! I make us nice chicken for nice lunch.'

'I can't,' I say. I'm getting a bit nervous.

'But I already prepare chicken now, and I have nice bottle of Hungarian wine also. Just come over.'

Out of the corner of my eye I watch Pierre getting up, wrapping himself in a towel. His eyes linger on my body, then he comes to me, kisses my back. I move away from Pierre while Laszlo keeps talking.

'OK, I'll see you in about an hour and a half,' I say and hang up.

Out of the window, on the street corner, I see a group of boys have just come out to play football. One of them is about ten years old and has a face like Wayne Rooney. He kicks the ball aggressively. Everyone is screaming; a Bangladeshi mother stands in front of her door shouting something to her children, her voice swept away by the noise of a rubbish collection truck. The day is starting.

In the bathroom, I hear Pierre having a shower. Downstairs, his two flatmates are wheeling out their bikes, closing the door and dashing off to work.

I sit down on the bed and dial my language school's number. Very sorry, I can't make it today, I say. I tell the receptionist that I have woken up with a fever and am going to try to sleep it off.

9.05 a.m.

I stand under the shower washing my hair. The water is suddenly very cold. I'm freezing. That dumb boiler has run out of hot water again. And in this flat even the cold water is lousy.

It's like living in the Third World. Then I can't find any soap. So I use shampoo to wash myself. I'm still new to Pierre's place; one week is not enough to get to know a house. And one month of being with Pierre is also not enough to know him. From that very first moment when I spotted him playing in a concert at the Barbican until now, I know no more about him except his brown guitar and silver recording machine by his bed.

Pierre doesn't really care how the flat looks – all of his stuff is in the wrong place. His shoes and CDs share the same shelf, and his violin is hanging in the wardrobe alongside his jeans. He also has a flute, which he told me he bought in Istanbul some years ago. He says he really worships it, but then I saw his flute leaning in a dusty corner of the room, with the broom and dustbin beside it. Before I met Pierre, I thought that composers were very clean and tidy people, except for the punk ones. Pierre is certainly not a punk, but he isn't tidy at all. I wonder whether I should help him – buy some new shelves for him, and clear out his collection of three hundred used plastic razors.

9.35 a.m.

Pierre has made coffee, and bread is in the toaster. He has also bought some goat's cheese from a nearby French deli. Pierre always complains he can't find good cheese in London, and when he occasionally does it costs the price of a cinema ticket. I don't care about cheese – I think it's a bit crazy to talk about cheese all the time, it's like talking about cow's tits. I don't really care about bread either. Brown or white, what's the difference? It's all made from the same crops. I'm Chinese. We eat better stuff than that.

I drink my cup of black coffee and bite into the goat's cheese. The coffee is so strong that immediately my intestines start to tremble. After the fifth sip, I have to run to the toilet. Pierre puts more coffee and water in the espresso machine, and turns on the gas again.

When I come back he's making an omelette. He always makes a big fuss about breakfast. If he makes an omelette, it won't be just a simple one, he will add courgette mash, or feta cheese. His omelettes taste very juicy, I have to admit. Pierre is very serious about food. He pays as much attention to each meal as he does to his music.

9.49 a.m.

While we eat, we listen to *September Songs* by Kurt Weill. Before I lived with Pierre, the only Western musician I knew was Elvis Presley. I rarely listened to any European music, and I'd certainly never wanted to hear German noise first thing in the morning. But for the last week I have been listening to Kurt Weill's songs every day. I am really drawn to the piece called 'September Song'. It makes my mind drift in a smoky shape – I can see an autumn forest spreading out in front of our misted kitchen window.

'Why do you like this one so much?' Pierre asks.

'I don't know. Maybe it's something to do with the East,' I say. I don't really know what I mean.

'To do with the East?' Pierre looks at me. 'How?'

I gulp down another mouthful of coffee. My intestines are still struggling in a dark world. He finishes his omelette. Now a German woman with a shrill voice starts to sing.

'Who is that? Sounds terrible.' I stop eating.

'It's Lotte Lenya, Kurt Weill's wife,' says Pierre.

'Why does his wife also have to sing a song?' I can feel myself getting annoyed.

Pierre laughs. 'No, she is a very good singer. This is called 'Pirate Jenny', it's about a working-class woman who dreams of becoming the wife of a great pirate.'

I try to like the song, but it's too dramatic for me. And outside the window the autumn forest disappears, washed away by a piercing female voice.

'I like Lotte Lenya,' Pierre says.

I say nothing. I can't be bothered. I put the last bit of omelette in my mouth; it suddenly tastes very salty. I spit it out. Perhaps Pierre was distracted by the German song while he was cooking. Now he digs out a new CD – another Lotte Lenya album. He plays me a song called 'Matrosen-Tango'.

'This is about a group of bourgeois men and women on a sinking boat before they reach Burma.'

The music is like a tropical typhoon, or a speeded up Italian opera. I try to draw a map of Asia in my brain to picture Burma's location; I can see big tigers living in a wild Burmese jungle, walking slowly and heavily.

Pierre pours me some more coffee. I am getting really restless.

'Stop! That's enough!' I scream.

Pierre stops pouring and looks at me, surprised.

'Too much stuff going on in the morning,' I complain. 'No more coffee and sugar, please, and no more omelettes either.' I look inside my chest. I see a greasy heart smothered by fat and protein, unable to beat freely. Perhaps I need to pump my chest to force my heart to beat continously. Pierre bursts out laughing. He stands up and pours the rest of the coffee into the sink. I hug him from behind. Pierre turns towards me and we kiss again.

'We didn't make love this morning,' he says.

'I know, but I am late.'

'So I officially invite you to make love when you come back tonight.'

'OK,' I say. I put on a pearl necklace.

Pierre looks at me. 'You said you didn't like that necklace.'

'Well, sometimes I like it.' I find a comb and put it into my bag.

It is not usual for me to use a comb. I don't comb my hair. I have very straight hair. But today, I need it.

11.20 a.m.

The Underground isn't as crowded as usual – I am late today and the morning rush hour is over.

There are only a few people in the carriage: on my left a

154

Muslim woman covered completely in black apart from her eyes, on my right an Englishman reading the *Sun*, with two naked blondes on page 3 – a bonus. Then hippy tourists in baggy trousers travelling with large backpacks. No one talks, everyone is secretive but bored and tired; but the train engines roar loudly today.

I take out my comb and start to brush my hair. It is still wet. I normally don't comb it, unless there's a special occasion, but I know Laszlo cares about how a woman looks. Perhaps that's the only thing Laszlo does care about in a woman.

The Tube ride is a boring one. I study the faces as strands of my broken black hair fall on the floor. People look at me inquisitively. A foreigner, some Chinese person who doesn't consider the environment, or an illegal Chinese immigrant.

I contemplate the comb in my hand while people move in and out of the carriage. I think I prefer to stay inside so I can avoid seeing the outside world. I don't like the outside world.

12.04 pm.

Laszlo is standing outside Notting Hill Gate station.

There are a few people waiting outside, but Laszlo is by far the most handsome. I spot him at once. He is tall and pale – that kills me. For some reason I like boys who have pale faces. Despite there being no sunlight, he is wearing a pair of rock-star sunglasses. He is leaning on a railing, and he smiles at me. His hair has grown much longer than it was a year ago. He wears dark jeans and a T-shirt with a big yellow orchid printed on it. The flower looks very inviting, and my heart starts to shake as I walk towards it.

Laszlo is a fashion designer. I'd never known anyone from Hungary before, let alone a Hungarian fashion designer. I don't really know if there is fashion in Hungary. All I had ever heard about Hungary is that they eat spicy beef stew constantly. That's it. Maybe Laszlo needs to be in London to do something fun – to meet truly fashionable people in late-night clubs, to watch skinny models parade on the catwalk, to drink cocktails with pop stars in trendy bars. We used to be lovers, but maybe 'lover' is too serious a word. We didn't love each other, that's the thing, but we liked making love together. Laszlo was going out with lots of different girls at the same time as he was seeing me. We would talk about it from time to time – I was his three-week-affair. I remember vividly how we used to make love during those three weeks. Of course, at that time I hadn't met Pierre yet, and I was still living with my previous boyfriend, Patrick. But all that time I was thinking of leaving Patrick. Then one afternoon – our last afternoon together – after Laszlo and I had made love, I told him that I was thinking of moving out of my boyfriend's place. 'No, you don't!' Laszlo sounded very worried. He didn't contact me for a long time after that.

I have been thinking of my mistake, the mistake I made with those men. Maybe I should listen more carefully to *Woman's Hour* on BBC Radio 4 each morning, and learn how to be a modern woman – a woman who believes in independence, and has the capacity to juggle a family and a career.

But I am the opposite of that. I am dependent, like a barnacle upon a rock.

'Wow, you looking great! Nice to see you,' Laszlo says to me.

'So do you,' I say. 'I like the orchid on your chest.'

Just like any normal friends, we kiss each other on the cheek. It feels strange. His cheeks are as cold as December.

As we walk side by side through Portobello Market, I keep thinking about Hungary – his country, and yet a country I know nothing about. I have seen it on European maps and I remember that there is no sea around it, only plains. Hungarian Plains. Maybe the colour of the soil is like the Hua Pei Plains in China – brown and grey. For that, I feel sad for Laszlo. But I don't want to say this to him.

12.37 p.m.

The wooden floor of Laszlo's house is painted white. It looks fashionable, but a bit cold hearted. Outside the glass door, the back garden is wild and the weeds are growing messily and lush. Dead leaves and vines cover the soil.

I open the back door and step onto the scattered leaves. A black cat jumps in from the neighbours' wall and stares at me, a small ghost.

'I am too lazy to make tidy garden,' Laszlo says, standing behind me.

'Of course, you haven't visited London for a year,' I say. Leaving the cat to roam the garden, I go back inside.

A pause. He says: 'Actually I visited London before, but I didn't call you.' He follows me back into the kitchen. I hear the cat miaow.

'You like some tea?' Laszlo puts on the kettle.

His house hasn't changed much since the last time I was here – there are just a few more oversized fashion magazines on the cold floor.

Alone, I walk upstairs. His bedroom is like a hotel room designed by a special interior decorator, everything is perfectly white and carefully arranged – velvet white lilies in a vase, milky-coloured curtains block the sunlight. His bed is as broad as an experimental theatre stage, and there are at least six pillows on it. I imagine an executive suite in a Novotel would look like this. I stare at the bed, picturing some six-foot model lying there last night. I mean, what do people do after fashion show parties? Laszlo definitely knows what to do. Jesus appears on a woollen rug hanging on the wall. I have never understood whether it's a religious display or a piece of artwork. I never dared ask Laszlo.

A huge bathtub stands in the middle of the bedroom. I've always been amazed by this tub – I love the idea of having a long lie in it. I'm sure there would be plenty of hot water in Laszlo's boiler, unlike Pierre's. But Laszlo has never offered me a bath – perhaps he is worried that I might stay at his place longer than the usual two hours. As I am contemplating the bathtub, Laszlo comes up to me, holding two cups of tea. I take one.

'How are you?' Laszlo asks, as though we haven't already

been together for nearly an hour. I don't know where to start.

'It's a bit of a mad time just now. I moved out of my ex-boyfriend's house, eventually…'

'Yes, I remember you talk about that.' Laszlo sips his tea.

'And now I live with a new man,' I continue.

'Oh, really?' Laszlo looks at me, surprised. He holds his mug with both hands, almost sheltering it.

'Yeah, we like each other a lot. His name is Pierre.'

I blow on the hot tea. Laszlo blows on his too.

'That's good, I guess,' he says.

We stand in the middle of the snow-white bedroom. There aren't any chairs nearby, only the bed. Laszlo's room is the opposite of Pierre's: in Pierre's bedroom there are stacks of practical items for our everyday life – it's like living in a compact supermarket.

'I did not think you find new man so quick.' Laszlo looks at me indifferently.

'Not so quickly really. I haven't seen you for a year. Things change.'

'So he is nice?'

'Yes.' I pause and then in a lighter tone say, 'Yes, he's all right.'

'Not English, no?'

'No, he's French.' Laszlo doesn't say anything. 'So what about you? Any new lovers in Budapest?'

Laszlo looks up at the Jesus on the wool rug, as if he should answer instead. A few seconds later, he says: 'Actually, I was about to be marry last month.' I turn to look at him. It's so

159

quiet, I can hear my heart beating in my chest. 'Then I decided not. It would be stupid,' Laszlo says in a low voice.

'But…why stupid?'

'I want my freedom, and also, I only…like her, but I don't love.'

Love. Laszlo has never mentioned this word to me. How difficult it is for people to get this word out of their mouths.

'Who is she?'

'You don't know her. She is underwear designer.'

What to say? I don't know anyone who designs underwear, I can't imagine anyone spending every day designing knickers and bras.

I look around the room, trying to find something to say.

'Lots of space here, though. You know, at Pierre's, we share the flat with another couple, our only private space is the bedroom, the whole place is only a little bigger than your bed.' Laszlo gazes at his large bed, then he looks away.

'Anyway then, how is your heart feeling?' Laszlo asks with a strong accent. I am surprised to hear his question – I don't know if he really cares about my heart.

'My heart is OK; actually it is a little happier than before,' I answer. 'How about yours?'

'My heart…a bit lonely,' he says.

'But how come? You always have someone.'

'Not really. Not now.'

I look at Laszlo, then at his unmade bed. So no six-foot girl lay there last night then. I feel a little embarrassed by my presumptions.

160

Laszlo walks around his room, reaching out to touch his bathtub, his table, then the curtains, as if he is a stranger in this house.

'Would you like to live with someone, or do you prefer to be alone?' I ask, my eyes following him.

'I don't really know,' he replies, in a melancholy mood.

I always assume Laszlo wants to be alone, because, without fail, after dating a girl for a few months he runs away. He puts his tea on the table, and comes towards me. Slowly, he presses his lips on mine. Then our lips stick together. It is a familiar feeling between me and him; our kisses have always been very indifferent.

1.41 p.m.

'So what about that chicken?' I say and cut him off. I walk towards the stairs, hoping to smell something from the oven.

'What chicken?' he says. Laszlo follows me, sniffing my neck and my hair like a dog.

'The chicken you talked about on the phone,' I say, annoyed. 'You said you'd cook it for me.'

'Yes, right. The chicken.'

'So?'

'It's in fridge,' he answers.

'But you said it was already prepared.'

'Well, it be prepare quick. Only take half one hour.'

'You just want to get me into your bed straight away. You don't care about anything else.' I suddenly feel angry.

The stairs are steep and narrow, but Laszlo stops me there and kisses me again. My neck begins to ache. I push him away, and walk down to the kitchen. Laszlo follows me.

By the kitchen table stacks of cookery books are displayed on a white shelf – how to make cakes, how to cook fish. What kind of fish swims in a Hungarian lake? I wonder.

Then I see Laszlo's wig, lying beside the books. 'You still have your wig,' I say. 'Do you wear it?'

'Yes,' he answers, 'for parties I wear. Last night I wore it and girls like me a lot.'

Laszlo takes the blonde wig from the vase, and puts it on. Now he's like a pop singer from the eighties, or some kind of oddly gentle punk. 'Do I look more attractive?' Laszlo makes a face and turns his head in all directions.

I sit on the sofa. The air in the house gets thicker and heavier, as if every piece of furniture had been soaked in camomile for months. I can't breathe freely and I'm getting sleepy. I feel like closing my eyes.

'I don't like Hungarians,' I say, in a bad mood.

'Why? You not even know any.' Laszlo comes to the sofa and sits beside me with his blonde wig messily tickling my neck.

'Well, I get a good idea from you and I think I don't like them.'

'But how can you say you don't like without know them?' Laszlo asks.

'I can feel.'

'You feel what?'

'I feel Hungarians are stupid.'

'I feel Chinese are dumb.'

Laszlo pulls my shoulder towards him forcefully and starts kissing me. His fingernails are almost embedded in my skin. It hurts.

2.05 p.m.

Laszlo is buried underneath my skirt. His beard makes my thighs itch and I start to laugh. I lift my skirt, I play with his wig.

It's getting very warm, and I feel sweat prickle on my skin. For a long time I can see only his blonde wig. It feels strange, as if I was being kissed by some blonde Danish girl. Laszlo gets up, removes my underwear but leaves my skirt on.

I'm getting hungry, the breakfast omelette has gone to the bottom of my stomach. I miss Pierre, and I feel guilty that I complained about his bread and coffee. Now I have to eat something urgently. All I can think of is food.

Suddenly I grow impatient. I push Laszlo to the floor, and hastily take off my skirt. I sit on top of his face. Laszlo is a bit surprised, but he obeys and remains quiet. After holding my hips and licking me for a while, he speaks from between my legs.

'Shall we go upstairs?' His voice is gentle, as if he is negotiating with me. I guess he doesn't want to annoy me. I carry on sitting on his face, without moving. 'Shall we go to the bedroom?' he insists.

'No. Why?'

I move my lower body and unzip his jeans. I take out his sex. It is hard, erect like a clay sculpture. I hold it tightly, so tightly that it must be painful for Laszlo. But perhaps he deserves it; it is revenge for what he started this morning on the phone. Pressing him into the floor, I start to rub him. His face becomes vague. And his breath grows heavier.

2.36 p.m.

I feel disgusted. This is meaningless. I'm bored. My body is bored. A few hours ago I was lying beside another body, Pierre's, the body which is slowly becoming my home. Now, beside Laszlo's, I start to feel cold.

I stand up and look at my clothes on the floor. Laszlo is not aware of my shift. He rises up and takes off his orchid-print T-shirt. He sits on the sofa, kissing my breasts. I wish he could move faster, it all takes too long.

As he sucks my nipples, I look at the glass lampshade above my head – it has a very odd shape, not round, not square, not triangular, it's like a melted ice cream on a plate. I look over at the table and picture a big juicy meal laid out. There is a pan of steamed rice and a dish piled high with roasted dumplings. I can almost smell the fragrant spices. My stomach growls.

I finally say in a very clear voice: 'Listen, I'm starving.'

'We'll eat soon.' He carries on sucking my breasts.

'I need to eat something now!'

Laszlo stops and studies my face. I stare at him, cold-hearted.

He stands up and his jeans slip to the floor. He doesn't give a damn about nakedness, and neither do I.

'Come and look here, what do you think?' He opens the fridge, his penis sticking out. I walk towards him and take a look at the freezer: a frozen chicken wrapped in plastic, covered in ice. 'It will take cooking only thirty minutes, or maximum forty minutes,' Laszlo claims, taking out his frozen chicken.

'There's no way you can get that done in thirty minutes, you haven't even defrosted it yet.'

'Defrost.' Laszlo repeats the word, but still studies his icy chicken.

'Forget it. Let's go out and find somewhere to eat,' I say, and walk towards my clothes. Laszlo throws the chicken back into the freezer.

2.56 p.m.

We walk through Kensal Green Cemetery. For years Laszlo has treated this graveyard as his own back garden, because his house is right next door.

'Don't you think I have best private garden in all London?' Laszlo is very proud of it.

'Do you have your own graveyard in Budapest too?' I tease him.

'I wish I did,' Laszlo answers, seriously.

It is like we are suddenly in the countryside. Wild flowers are blooming, grass and bushes are lush and heavy. Here and there, I see new marble crosses standing on old gravestones, like a new hat on an old man's head. Other graves are in pieces, sinking into the soil, covered in moss and nearly invisible.

Laszlo points to a stone.

JOSEPH CHAMBERS 1792–1843

It's Mr Chambers' only remnant in this world.

'I never realised people from two hundred years ago were buried here,' I say.

'Why not?'

Laszlo carelessly walks on the grave, his shoes leaving streaks of mud on the carved date.

'Who decided to put a cemetery in the middle of the city?' I murmur to myself.

Laszlo shrugs his shoulders. 'And why you think not? It is very normal,' he says.

For Laszlo, nothing is unusual. Maybe that's why he has suddenly called me to come over after a year of no contact at all. I remember he used to say that he was an existentialist. An existentialist never thinks anything is unusual because everything exists without reason. And I told him that in universities in China existentialism means something different – it means people want to be lazy. That was perhaps one of the last conversations I had with Laszlo.

'You think they should move graveyard to suburb then? Just like Chinese government with old houses?' Laszlo asks sardonically. I don't comment. 'I heard news that Chinese government even wants to move Forbidden City to suburbs in Beijing. They want to create same-size replica. Is true?'

Trampling over the wild weeds, I walk faster and faster, so Laszlo has to run after me. There's no one around; it is so quiet only the birds are chirping. I breathe in the cool air and feel much happier. Laszlo puts his arm around me, starting to talk about some martial arts film he watched recently – *The Adventures of Iron Pussy*. I laugh because of the name Iron Pussy, and I say I always fall asleep when I watch martial arts films.

'But don't Chinese like watch martial arts films?' Laszlo asks.

'Of course, you would think that.'

We cross the street outside the cemetery and spy a few restaurants on the road ahead.

'Which one you prefer?' Laszlo asks me.

'I don't care – anywhere they cook quickly.'

I enter one of the small restaurants at random. There is only an old man eating a leg, maybe a chicken leg, with a pint of beer in front of him. Right away, I order some beef. 'Medium rare, please,' I say to the waitress.

Laszlo looks at the old man's plate. 'Can I have duck leg please, and also red orange juice?'

I don't understand how Laszlo can tell so easily that the cooked leg is definitely duck and not chicken. The waitress just nods in response.

Twenty seconds later, the waitress brings over two glasses of juice. She has big round breasts. Laszlo's eyes are glued to her.

'Enjoy,' she says, smiling at Laszlo.

'Thank you.' He smiles at her like a gentleman. I drink my juice in silence.

Laszlo's gaze comes back to me gradually. 'How is you teaching?'

'Busy. This year we have more students, and I'm not only teaching my classes, but also doing some as a private tutor. Everyone wants to do business with the Chinese now.'

'Are the students good?' Laszlo asks me, but his eyes are still following the waitress around the restaurant.

'Not really. When they study, they always want to find the logic behind the Chinese language, but we Chinese aren't logical. Then they ask why aren't the Chinese logical? But we just aren't. I tell them all they need do is to recite what they learn like they recite the Bible. But they don't believe that. Sometimes I wonder whether they'll ever learn.'

'Well, don't be so hard, they are just stupid Westerners like me.' Laszlo sips his orange juice.

The food arrives. From the size of the leg, it must have been a really big duck. Laszlo devours his lunch. I am now too hungry to eat, my stomach clenches badly. I've lost my appetite.

'It's as if they learn Chinese for me, not for themselves,' I carry on complaining.

'Oh well, Chinese is so difficult language, everybody know that. That's why I don't agree people say Chinese as universal language next century. It's not possible.'

Laszlo shakes his head, and puts another piece of duck meat into his mouth. The old man nearby finishes his duck leg and starts to read the *Independent* – Vladimir Putin is on the cover, his eagle eyes watching us eating.

4.11 p.m.

Walking back through the graveyard, we pass our old friend Joseph Chambers. Mr Chambers lived for fifty-one years. I wonder how he died. Perhaps he was a priest; I imagine that every Western man was a priest in the early nineteenth century, just as any Chinese man had to be a peasant growing crops in the fields. Life was simple.

To get to the Tube station, I have to pass Laszlo's house.

'Will you come for coffee before you leave?' Laszlo asks and looks at me, an ambiguous expression on his face.

'No, I think I should go back home.' I walk faster.

'Just quick coffee. Then go,' he insists.

'No, I don't want to.'

'Just five minutes.' He takes my hand in his. 'I don't know when I see you next,' he adds. I suddenly feel sad. I decide this will be the last time in my life that I see Laszlo. I swear I don't want to see him ever again.

4.36 p.m.

The kettle is boiling, and instant coffee is waiting in the cups on the kitchen table. Since I have been seeing Pierre, I never drink instant coffee. He hates it. But I don't say that to Laszlo.

Lying naked on the sofa, I let Laszlo caress my body. I am a bit worried about the boiling kettle, but Laszlo doesn't seem to care. I listen to the water boiling and watch the steam rising from the lid in a thin cloud. My mobile starts to beep in my bag. It must be Pierre; he knows my class finishes at four.

The phone is silent for a few minutes, then beeps again. I'm getting nervous. I can't pretend any more, and I don't need any crappy instant coffee either. I really am in a hurry. But I know Laszlo will want to carry on with his plan. He will not let me go so easily.

The kettle switch eventually flicks off. It must be Joseph Chambers having mercy on me.

'Take off your jeans,' I say. Laszlo takes off his jeans. 'Your shirt too.' He takes off his orchid shirt.

When he's completely naked, I stand up from the sofa, and tell him to lie down. I sit right on top of Laszlo's erect penis. I feel the pain when he enters my body. I see Laszlo feels uneasy too, but he doesn't say anything. He tries to cooperate. My lower body hurts; I carry on banging him hard, up and down. Laszlo moans, maybe he feels pain too. I don't know.

I turn round and lie on his chest. Laszlo grabs me, and penetrates me from behind. It is so hard and tight, like a nail being banged into the wall. There is nothing beautiful or good but the pain. He withdraws from inside me, and comes. Sperm flows everywhere, trickling down between his thighs.

5.57 p.m.

Laszlo walks with me to the Tube station, our bodies exhausted – we have no words to say to each other. By the time we reach Notting Hill Gate, my stomach is aching like crazy.

I can't walk. I stop in the middle of the pavement, and wait for the pain to go.

'I'm sorry,' Laszlo says.

'It's not your fault.' I kneel down on the ground.

'It was very painful for me; it must be more worse for you,' Laszlo murmurs.

I can't talk. I can't move one more centimetre or my loins will break and my stomach cramp like hell. I think I'm going to die here. I'm close to the graveyard, and I can almost see my fresh gravestone in the ground. I suddenly think of my friend Joseph Chambers lying under the soil for 150 years.

'You want to go back and lie down a bit?'

'No.'

Laszlo looks at me, and this time he starts to worry. 'Maybe we walk a bit in my graveyard? It's quiet – might help.'

'No. Please.'

I stand up again, concentrating on pushing the tide of pain away from my body. I walk down the stairs into Notting Hill Gate Tube station. Laszlo follows me. As I search for my ticket, Laszlo watches a girl in a tight skirt passing in front of us.

'Let me know tonight you OK. Call me,' Laszlo says. Then he kisses me on the lips.

'I will be fine...when I get home.'

People push me from behind like crazy, it's rush hour again. Office workers, students, men and women, old and young, all flooding into the Underground. Shoulders bump against each other, hair tickles strangers' faces. I stand on the platform in the middle of it all. It smells terrible, I feel dizzy. The moment when the train passes in front of me, vomit spits out of my mouth.

6.45 p.m.

I walk down Fennel Street. Council houses. There are rubbish bins and piles of junk everywhere. It's getting dark, and the street lights are on. I feel down. I don't know exactly where I should go. I miss my old life with Patrick. And I miss Patrick badly. It's a feeling like the stomach ache, but this ache doesn't go away just like that. It stays there, it hurts just when you think it has stopped.

Patrick's house is only two streets away from Pierre's. For the last three years, I've been walking down Fennel Street with my shopping bag or my umbrella every day. For the last three years, I didn't know that there was a man called Pierre living only two streets away, and that one day I'd end up leaving Fennel Street and moving to be with him.

Since I moved out of his house, I think of Patrick more than ever. I think of him especially when I lie in bed with Pierre, even when we are listening to the great Kurt Weill. Pierre knows I am thinking of Patrick, but he doesn't say anything – he waits. Maybe he believes time is a black hole that will swallow everything, including memories. So why worry?

Patrick is a carpenter. I don't know how he spends his days since I left. He told me that he could feel very lonely, even when I was with him in a room. I never understood that.

When he works, he doesn't talk to anyone, no chat, no music, no phone calls. He is a loner. And most of the time we were together I would sleep whilst he was working.

I stop in the middle of Fennel Street. I still have the key to Patrick's house. I need to see him. I have to. I will feel calm again when I see Patrick, even if it makes him sad to see me now.

7.39 p.m.

118 Fennel Street. Quiet and desolate as it ever was. Only pieces of half-finished woodwork on the floor; no one is around.

Patrick has been living here for several years. He is always making things – doors, shelves, floors, fences. At the moment there are some half-made windows leaning on the wall, no glass yet. Sawdust is spread on the floor.

As I walk upstairs the shadow of my earlier pain makes my stomach cramp and shudder. I want to see our bed, the bed which now holds only his body. The sheets are messy, a blue shirt lies on the duvet, some pages of the *Guardian* scattered about. This bed is starting to assume a bachelor's shape. The shape of carelessness. I see his radio, his only entertainment before he sleeps. Wet socks and jeans are hung by the window; maybe he has just done the laundry this afternoon.

I open a small wardrobe, the one Patrick made for me when I first moved in. It's made from abandoned wood from a rubbish dump, and I painted it lemon yellow. A beautiful piece of furniture. But now the inside is empty, only an old black bra that had lost its elasticity, and a pair of torn stockings. I don't remember the last time I wore stockings, I never liked them. Neither Patrick nor Pierre liked stockings, so I stopped buying them.

On the kitchen table: a dried tea bag in a teacup and some onions on the chopping board. In an open pot there is some cooked porridge. Patrick, like many other English people, is a vegetarian. He doesn't even eat omelettes, while I eat only meat. I wonder if that's one of the reasons why we split up.

I remember when we were together Patrick would spend a lot of time in his garden. He loved digging the soil and setting out new plants, while I only like to look at the flowers. And now I miss his garden. I open the back door, switch on the light. I know every plant here, I know their stories. New mint leaves are coming out, and the lemongrass is growing strong. The vines are lush. No dead trees, no wilted leaves. A gust of wind comes in, blowing the heavy, over-bloomed roses.

I close the back door and walk into the kitchen towards an old blue table. I liked working at that table, it faces the garden window and I used to be able to see the cloudy sky from there. It looks like Patrick hasn't used it since I left. Only my stapler remains – lonely on the blue wood. I open the drawers one by one – there are some of my papers, some mobile phone bills. I stare at them, wondering whether I should take them with me to Pierre's. Then I discover my passport hiding underneath. I'm surprised, I thought the first thing I did when I moved out was to pack my passport. How could I forget that? How could

Patrick have not mentioned it to me either? I skim through my passport, Chinese stamps, one page after another. I put it in my pocket and close the drawer.

On Patrick's table there are some nails and tools. Then there is his diary, open.

6 FRIDAY
Mary Hackney City Farm 6.30

7 SATURDAY
Penny's birthday

8 SUNDAY
Shepherd's Bush Charity mtg

Patrick is an organised and patient person; everything he does takes time. He kept telling me I needed a diary to keep myself organised. But I don't know what for. I just live, live randomly. I want to be free from plans, free from tomorrow, and mostly I prefer to sleep or do nothing.

I put the kettle on, sit on a chair, waiting. I don't know if I'm waiting for Patrick or just for the water to boil. I touch the passport in my pocket, and that makes me feel calm.

8.57 p.m.

There is a half-moon in the sky, but no stars. The moonlight is weak, as pale as Laszlo's face.

175

As I open the door, I can hear the sound of French being spoken, and the noisy extractor fan on in the background. Mozart is playing from Pierre's expensive stereo. I know Pierre doesn't totally hate Mozart, but he wouldn't choose to listen to him in the kitchen. I think perhaps there are old people in the house.

True enough, an elderly couple are in the kitchen, arguing in French about something in the saucepan. The pan is sizzling, the gas flame strong. Pierre stands beside them, listening to their argument, without taking sides.

'Hello,' I interrupt.

'Oh, here you are!' Pierre screams when he sees me. 'This is my mum and dad, this is Yu Shu.'

'Hello, how are you?' His mother smiles at me.

'Very nice to meet you,' his father says and hugs me warmly.

I had no idea what Pierre's parents looked like – they have dark suntanned skin and speak loudly.

'Nice to meet you, and…welcome,' I say.

Pierre makes Mozart a little quieter. 'I phoned you this afternoon, wanted to let you know they'd be coming tonight, but I couldn't get through.'

His mother dries her hands on our flatmate's hand towel while talking to me. 'Sorry we arrived without any warning. We were in Italy for two weeks, and at the last minute we decided to visit London. We thought we would surprise Pierre. I hope you don't mind.'

'Yes, and we're going back to Avignon tomorrow,' his father says.

'You are very welcome to stay,' I answer.

I find a glass, and drink some water. I wonder if they know that I have only been living here for a week. I, too, am a guest in this house.

The mother seems to know this kitchen very well. She opens the cupboard and takes out four plates, then gets four pairs of knives and forks.

'I'm sorry I'm late…I went to Oxford Circus, and I got carried away,' I say, taking out a bottle of red wine from the plastic bag.

'But did you get my message?' Pierre asks.

'I was on the Tube.' I turn to his parents. 'I bought some cheese as well.' I take out two small goat's cheeses.

'*Oh, c'est bon!*' Pierre's mother exclaims.

'*Parfait!*' Pierre's father says.

'Great. OK, dinner is ready.' Pierre arranges four wine glasses on the table.

I'm exhausted. My eyes hurt. I miss my bed. I could sleep right away. I take off my pearl necklace and throw it on the corner of the table. I take out the comb from my bag too.

I hug Pierre very briefly, and I can feel my passport is still safe in my pocket.

'I've missed you,' he says. He caresses my hair, and his parents watch us from behind him. We quickly free ourselves from the embrace.

His father and mother now both concentrate on the saucepan. The mother grinds some black pepper into it.

Pierre brings the hot pan to the table. There's a big sea bass surrounded by roasted green and red peppers. The fish's eyes are vivid, staring up at us.

Everyone sits down. Pierre's father opens the wine, and pours it into the glasses.

'Cheers.' Everyone raises their glasses, smiles at me with their big eyes wide open.

Pierre reminds me to look into people's eyes when I chink their wine glasses. He was surprised to hear I had never done that before. I told him that we Chinese don't look into people's eyes unless they are our enemies. And I don't want more enemies.

I watch the steam rising from the shiny fish flesh.

'Cheers,' I say. I raise my eyes. I look at the three of them.

I drain the wine and fearfully return his parents' smiles, and start to eat the sea bass. It tastes extremely good and everyone praises it.

Pierre's mother raises her glass to toast a second time, and then suddenly the electricity goes off. The whole flat is plunged into darkness. Pierre whistles and his parents gasp. They immediately switch to speaking French.

I hear Pierre rising from his chair, rummaging around trying to find some candles. I close my eyes; rest my heavy head on the corner of the table, sink into the darkness and at once I fall asleep.

LETTERS TO A CITY OF
ILLUSION AND HOPE

Letter to H

I am writing to you from Berlin. I know you will be surprised
to hear from me – I guess you would never have imagined that
I would write to you. But for some strange reason you
appeared in my dream last night – it was vivid, strange and so
real. And I woke up this morning wondering how you are.

I was the customer you always saw around midnight. The
woman who arrived alone, wearing a pair of green sandals,
always with a book in her hand. Sometimes I fell asleep while
you were massaging me. I would constantly argue with you
saying you should be studying at university not working in a
massage parlour. You were by far the cleverest boy there.

I was staggered when you told me that your whole village
had left the countryside for large cities to work in the massage

business. How many people were there in your village? Three thousand? Or thirty thousand? You said yours was the most populated province in China. I imagined thousands of young Henan villagers leaving their homes, waiting on train platforms with their luggage, fighting for a place – only to come to work in the smoggy Beijing streets massaging city people's feet. So, you all came to Beijing and Shanghai to press and pummel tired feet, day and night. So many feet – and maybe you remember some of those feet, but certainly not their faces.

You were seventeen then. I was spending all day every day writing scripts, arguing with fellow film-makers. I was absorbed in my world. It was overwhelming and noisy and hectic. I think you told me once that you'd like to be an actor, you were good at martial arts, and you'd like to leave your job and act in a TV series. I gave you a phone number for a film studio and told you to call them. And then I never saw you again. I hoped I'd bump into you one day walking out of a film studio, discussing your latest stunt with some hotshot director. Sometimes, I miss those quiet, solitary nights we spent together while the whole city was asleep.

Letter to G

In your last letter you said you didn't like Berlin, and didn't want to stay here any longer than you had to. You were so pleased to leave Germany, in spite of coming to see me for such a short visit. You said you didn't like the conceptual art produced by young artists that fills the white space in every Berlin gallery, you said you felt uncomfortable watching the lovers kissing in bars. Well, you have changed, my friend, changed a lot since I left China ten years ago.

Do you remember the winter of 1993, Beijing battered by Mongolian winds; you were eighteen and I was twenty. One night we were walking through the cold November air over Ji Men Bridge. People used to call that canal Little Moon River. The water was still flowing then, though I'm sure it was frozen that night. It was a dirty brown, littered with plastic bags and the detritus of the city. We never saw fish in the canal nor any boats. And the pine-tree wood near the riverbank – we would see lovers from the nearby art school creep out, holding hands or secretly kissing. No room for lovebirds to hide except for in the woods at night. What did we do? I can hardly remember. Where did we hide and kiss? It is so long ago now, my memory is hazy and filled with new thoughts, new smells and sounds and colours from all the years that have passed since. You were studying 1960s Paris and bursting with ideas – do you remember? Ah, how much exciting nonsense we learnt in our art-school library, perhaps the only place in Beijing where censorship on Western art didn't apply. You would talk about Sartre and de Beauvoir. Of course! In those days there was no stopping you talking about them. You lived so much in another time and another world, a world where men resembled the young Sartre and women the young de Beauvoir. You could only afford two packs of instant noodles each day; but the library was free. We were living through the ruthless sandy winds of Beijing: orphans of our country's history. We were born during the Cultural Revolution, my friend, and all we were taught was that History equals Feudalism. So history had to die. Do you recall those debates?

Now you say you are no longer interested in any of these things: literature, art, not even history. Here in Berlin there is the concrete history of buildings and streets – the scars of history that can't be forgotten or erased. You and I both know there is no history that can be found in Beijing anymore.

The year I left China you were writing a novel in the style of Jorge Luis Borges, and I was finishing a script for a TV soap to make some money to move to Germany. We stole cabbages in the hutongs; you borrowed money to buy cigarettes. We went through the cruel story of youth. Then one day you took me to a dim jazz cafe near Wudaokou, called Lush Life, right next to the Beijing Language College. You said they played the best jazz in town. We were the only ones in the audience. I think that was the first time I saw a black American jazz musician. I remember asking you why they would come to Beijing. Didn't they find life tough or lonely here? You said: they come here for the same reason that you are moving to Berlin – and will you find life tough and lonely there? I still have no answer to this question.

After those hot-headed Beijing days, I disappeared from the country and we disappeared from each other's lives. Shortly after I left China, I heard that the jazz cafe had disappeared too. They started demolishing all the winding streets in Beijing –

the small stalls in Wudaokou, the ones that sold the cheapest chilli paste and Korean kimchi, are all gone.

Now you tell me that you don't like that underground world any more. Now you tell me you prefer the life you have in Beijing – the clean streets, the expensive houses, the shopping centres and the shiny office blocks – because you have become a father and a husband perhaps? Has time proved to be so powerful, has memory proved to be so forgettable? Tell me, please, I cannot believe it is all forgotten so easily. And I hope, one day, you will revisit Berlin.

Letter to A

Can you do me a favour, my friend? Could you look up a girl I used to know? I want you to go and see her, if you can. Her name is Chiu Chiu and her address is 10th East Cheng De Road – you know the road, it's that one round the corner from the train station. She used to live in a hutong house, but it has been so long now.

She is small, but beautiful, or at least she used to be. I have not seen her for many years, and much can change in that time.

We liked the same sort of music – Miles Davis and Pink Floyd. We loved Eileen Chang's novels, and the same sort of films – all Billy Wilder movies – laughing loudly together. We even had the same kind of gestures, and a similarly shrieky voice. We spent all our time together. It feels so strange, you know, being so intensely involved with someone and then losing them completely. In Berlin I don't laugh the same way as I used to laugh in Beijing. I don't laugh much now.

I remember everyone thought she was my younger sister. She was a rebel. She had left her home town in Shangdong Province when she was just sixteen and came to Beijing to sing. At work and in bars she sang pop songs from Hong Kong and Taiwan – 'Goodbye my love' by Deng Lijun mixed with English words; propaganda songs too, in a Beijing Army dancing troupe. And she would even sing walking down the street – humming along to pop tunes – and in the market buying food, and on the bus coming home, and in the summer swimming in the lakes. I remember her boyfriend well – perhaps you'll also find him there. He was Beijinese and a singer too, and had a kind face. We three used to play ping-pong together, and he was, of course, always the champion of every game. She used to stay at his place a lot – that old hutong house nearby the train station – and eventually moved in. Then one day I went to see her in that windowless home. And each time a train departed we could hear the horns and bells clanging and the kitchen table shuddered. We ate lamb hotpot seasoned with anything she could find and mix together – shrimps, squid, chicken feet, seaweed, pig intestines. We sweated so much from the food that we opened the front door and watched the snow outside gradually covering the grey city. Their house was decayed, the cement walls stained by rain, covered with a large piece of flowery cloth. Silvery grey lilies danced up the crumbling wall. Hers was the dark house of grey lilies.

And I remember she would come and find me at my art school, in my dormitory room with bunk beds for four students, where a tall chimney vomited its black smoke out of our windows. I can picture that first day she visited me so vividly: she walked in confidently, one hand carrying dried duck meat in a greasy paper wrap, the other holding a book called Existentialism or Post-Marxism or something like that. She told me it had been written by a Harvard scholar – or was he from Berkeley? I don't remember any more, it doesn't matter now. It was all so new to me. I asked her whether she understood this heavy Western book. And she said, Of course, I have to. You know for our diploma we had to know about Heidegger and Roland Barthes; or at least know how to spell Nietzsche or Heraclitus, or even Alexanderplatz. How ridiculous it all was. We didn't even know where Germany was! But we were so young and earnest, so desperate to succeed. It would be good to laugh together again.

She decided that she wanted to change her life – she saw that being a singer in a little troupe was leading nowhere. She was full of energy and plans, she wanted to go abroad, to America, anywhere in America, no matter whether it was in Wisconsin or Oregon or Kentucky. At night we would go out and listen to punk bands play in a dark underground bar in Chao Yang district. Cui Jian was singing 'Rock and Roll on a New Long March' in a band of long-haired guys. And she was their favourite girl. She dyed her hair red, wore a shiny top and a pair of trousers with bell-bottomed elephant feet, and danced like a mad thing right next to the stage. Was that Elvis Presley style, or Hong Kong second-hand imitation?

Then one day I left Beijing to come to Berlin. She wrote to me: I am married, I am in Helsinki, and I miss Beijing. Her words worried me. And some months later I heard she had left Finland, where she could see the Northern Lights for half of the year. The winter evenings were too long for her, she said – through the sleepless nights she would read Chinese novels until the dawn brightened her window. Eventually she went back to her old Beijing. I hope you will find her there, if the house or the street still exist.

Letter to W

Sorry I haven't responded to your letters earlier. Somehow days pass unnoticed and I move through these months blindly. You asked me to send you photos of that well. Do you mean the well inside the Forbidden City, the well in which the Emperor's favourite concubine was drowned by the Emperor's own mother? I remember taking those photos. I've enclosed all of the ones I could find – it was strange looking at them again.

I suppose you still remember that trip we made to the Forbidden City? It felt like there was no museum in the world as empty as that one. OK, it wasn't entirely empty, but every gallery was locked. Where are all the treasures? we asked. The guards looked at us blankly, and so you whispered to me, they've probably all gone to Taiwan, to Taipei's Forbidden Palace, or maybe to the British Museum which has all the jade, the Buddhas, and the Emperor's golden quilt.

And like any other tourist from the Chinese provinces we took photos in front of that famous well, the Zhen Fei well. Its water seemed bottomless – I felt a rush of vertigo. You asked the guide if any tourists had fallen into it by accident. The guide promised us that it was all safely under control. We stood by the well and read out of our guidebook the story of how Emperor Guangxu's concubine Zhen Fei was killed by his mother. A depressing story. We were standing next to each other in complete silence looking down that stone well at the scrappy autumn leaves floating on dark water.

History is a big deal here in Berlin. The other day I was talking about the year 1900 with a group of Berliners. It was late, and we were eating kebabs in a Krentzberg cafe. I told them 1900 was the year of the Eight-Nation Alliance – Western armies entered China and Empress Cixi had to escape from Beijing in a crazy rush. They knew little about it, of course. I told them how the city was occupied, houses burnt down, citizens fled. Do you remember learning this at school? We learnt how Emperor Guangxu was in love with his unofficial concubine – Zhen Fei – against his mother's will. Cixi left the Emperor behind in Beijing to negotiate with the invaders, and ordered for Zhen Fei to be thrown into the well. The Emperor fled, the girl drowned. My friends looked horrified. But it's so recent, one of them said.

Then a man at the next table leaned over and started arguing in heated German that 'historically' the concubine Zhen Fei didn't drown in this exact well, it was somewhere else, perhaps not even in the Forbidden City – you would have laughed, he was so serious, so exact! I got angry – some idiot German scientifically educating me about my own country. For the confused Chinese tourists who have lost all trace of history in the Cultural Revolution what matters is only this: a beautiful concubine was drowned in a well for the sake of love, for her master, or perhaps to make history roll on like a tape recorder.

Looking at these photos now, I want to visit that well again – stand there and look down into the dark depths – or perhaps you can do that for me? Can you check whether the well is still there, or has it been moved to make way for a shiny Starbucks cafe? I hope the water has not dried up.

Letter to M

Every day I realise how much I miss you. Why is our time together always about coping with the next absence? And isn't it a joke, now that we have swapped our cities – you are in Beijing and I am in your hometown Berlin.

Tell me, what happened the last time we met? I was there – for you – waiting at Beijing airport in the middle of the night. Your flight was delayed, and it felt like I was waiting forever. I watched so many other flights come in – couples reunited, families laughing, tired and crumpled after long journeys. And I was there, curling up my stiff body on the plastic chair for two long hours. I got up and flicked through every magazine in the shop, ate a plate of tasteless airport noodles, and then I slept again on the hard chair. Eventually you appeared, with your indifferent smile. We rode home in the taxi with your red suitcase behind us. Holding hands in silence in the shaky taxi, the highway ride felt long and the road went on forever, as long as the time we had been separated. You gazed at the poplar trees standing straight and tall on the sides of the highway, silent in the darkness. Obedient forest, you murmured. Obedient forest – is that what you think of Beijing? Did you mean the obedience of its citizens, or its government? Or every tree, building, person?

In that red suitcase, you'd brought me an art book called *Griffin and Sabine*. I had never seen a foreign book before. It may have been a love story, but for me it was my first adult children's book. I had never read a children's book because I only ever heard propaganda stories when I was young.

Since then I've often thought of Griffin and Sabine's love – a man in London writing postcards to a woman on a mysterious island in the South Pacific. I remember wondering where in the South Pacific that island could be? In my tower-block apartment in Beijing, seventeen flights up, I stood on my bed and stared at the world map glued to my wall. I traced the green patches in the ocean of blue with my finger: was it Fiji? Samoa? Nauru? Or the Solomon Islands? Are there any mysterious islands left in this world?

And now I am in Berlin, trying to be with you – but you are not here any more. I find myself slowly becoming like the character in *Griffin and Sabine* – Griffin is so lonely that he has to invent this distant woman in his imagination. All I did in

Berlin in my first two years was just sit in the kitchen scribbling Chinese in my diaries, and watching the news on TV trying to guess what the reporters were saying in German. I became Griffin; Sabine is the lost me.

Now I am in a bedroom where out of my window I can see an avenue of linden trees. Today the sky is covered with heavy rainy clouds, and the stormy wind is blowing into my bedroom, blowing my world map pinned on the wall. I am looking at the map. I want to find that city again, a city with you in it, a city full of the hopes and illusions of our youth.

TODAY I DECIDE TO DIE

Today I decided to die. Friday, 3 July. There is nothing special about today, I haven't planned a particular day for dying. And I hadn't thought about my death before yesterday. Tomorrow is 4 July, Independence Day, as the Americans say. I only realised it this morning, when I arrived in Salt Lake City from Coalville. On every shop door there was a sign saying: *July 4th, closed for Independence Day*.

It feels like everything has started to close already though: the shops are empty, the shelves bare, the streets quiet with only the hum of occasional cars under the sharp, hard July sun. Everyone is at home with the family, raising their national flag on the front lawn. So is this America then?

My name is Zhang Yi, and Li Kai is my boyfriend, actually my fiancé. We got engaged in January, in Red Peach Park in our home town, and had a beautiful tea ceremony with all our family members. A week ago we flew from our province of Guang Xi with a guided tourist group to the state of Utah. We live in a very poor province, near the southern border of China, which the local authorities managed to make a sister province with Utah in the USA. But no one, including me, had even heard of Utah. And I really can't find any similarities between my home in Guang Xi and this big dusty flat place. We don't have cowboys or doughnut shops on the highways. All we have are a few pandas in our local zoo; the rest of our province is taken up by construction sites. Anyway, that's not the story I want to tell you. I want to tell you about Li Kai. He seems to know almost everything there is to know. He studied hybrid plantation initially at college, then did computing for his MA. In my father's words, he is a promising young man who knows the future of both agriculture and industry. At least we definitely won't starve in our life together.

This is our first time abroad. We studied the map of Utah endlessly before leaving China; and reviewed it again in the aeroplane as we looked down at the landscape below, starting to appear through the clouds. Our tour guide announced that we would walk on the Great Salt Lake, and climb up famous mountains, listen to country music in local bars, eat traditional American food and drink coffee at petrol stations in polystyrene cups. We thought we would meet the real old Americans: Indians, we were told – what a strange word to use for Americans, we thought, since India lies right next to China.

Our one-week tour didn't disappoint. For the first three

days, we were very excited and behaved like real peasant tourists from China; we stayed in a posh hotel at the bottom of a mountain, walked through a quiet valley along a river, and saw the famous Great Salt Lake. It was enormous, as big as the sea, gulls flying above the blue water exactly like in the picture in the brochure.

But after three days, Kai's enthusiasm faded away and he fell into a state of melancholy. He didn't speak a word to me, from breakfast until supper. This was not normal. Usually, Kai is a light-hearted person – he likes jokes and funny films, detective stories and sport; and I thought he liked travelling. But he stayed in the tour coach all the time, gloomy, not even coming down to take photos. I began to think that he didn't like America. Or maybe he hated eating sandwiches every day – surely he too was depressed by those strange leafy salads without any meat in them. Or perhaps he was missing our little house in Guang Xi. He behaved like this for the rest of the trip. On the last day of our tour – yesterday morning – he woke up, brushed his teeth for a long time, standing at the window staring out at the dusky blue American hills in the distance where Indians might have lived once. Then, still holding the toothbrush in his hand. And then, all of a sudden, he told me this: he had another woman in Shanghai. He didn't think our marriage would work. Furthermore, he said, after this US trip he was going to move to Shanghai to be with that woman. I'm in love with her, Zhang Yi, not with you, he said quietly. I'm sorry.

These are the exact words he spoke, standing by the bathroom door. He was so far away. I felt as if he was talking to me standing on a distant mountaintop opposite our hotel room.

Then last night my stomach began to ache. We slept together in the same bed, in the same room, exactly as we had done before. There was no breeze. No air came through the window, and we felt suffocated.

Suddenly, two wolf-like dogs are barking and running at me, and I see policemen following behind the dogs. It's all a blur. I am running my soul out – fast, faster, to get away. I sit up in bed; it is very dark. Kai is lying next to me, but facing the other side of the room. I can't make out if he is sleeping or thinking. I look at my watch; it is two in the morning. I feel unbearable. I get up, leave our bedroom and start walking around the dim hotel. This wooden house hotel is owned by a rich Mormon, and as I wander around late that night I see dozens of depressing paintings of Jesus on the wall – so many of them! We even had three Jesus paintings in our bedroom. The rest of the pictures on the walls are family photos. Mormons seem to have huge and healthy families – each photo was crowded with people, perhaps no one has died to make space for the younger people. And in the toilet, placed on a little table near an arse-washing seat, I found a black book entitled *Book of Mormon*. I didn't know whether this was compulsory reading for all Mormons, just like Chairman Mao's *Little Red Book* used to be for all Chinese people. I open the book at the introduction and read: 'We invite all men everywhere to read the *Book of Mormon*, to ponder in their hearts the message it contains, and then to ask God, the Eternal Father, in the name of Christ if the book is true.'

I feel desperate about things with Kai, I can't pull myself together to think about such a serious issue. I close the book, but it is so heavy that it falls into the toilet bowl. I fish it out and dry it with a towel. I try to mop the pages – but the bottom half of every single page is now stained with water – stained and soaking wet, for 428 pages, with the toilet flushing water.

Today, we are supposed to be flying back to China. When the coach arrives at the airport, Li Kai just follows the tour guide, pulling his suitcase behind him like all the other Chinese tourists. He doesn't pay any attention to me. Hastily, I jump into a taxi and tell the driver to drive away as fast as he can. I know everyone will be shocked to discover that I'm missing, I can picture Li Kai's astonished face in the plane back to China without me. But then, nothing can be more shocking than what he told me yesterday. When I think of going back to Guang Xi to carry on living in a house without my fiancé, I feel there is nothing to keep me in China any more.

Now that I'm alone and there is no guide telling me where to go and what to do in my life, I wander around with a foggy mind. Dragging my luggage behind me I arrive downtown. But I don't understand – is 'downtown' the south side of the town? Does that mean the north is always up, like on a map hanging on the wall? I can't think of a three-dimensional concrete city with only two dimensions, one up and one down. Seeing 'downtown' signs on every metal pole in the street only makes me more confused. Why are they there? Are they advertisements for some city development estate, like the 'Beijing 2008 Olympics' signs that were posted everywhere in China before the games? But why do I still care about these useless things anyway? While my mind denies my life, my eyes still absorb the world around me. This city is brand new, I've never, ever encountered a city as new as this one, not even in my province. Here, the buildings are made of marble, huge and tall, like respectful gravestones. The windows are all closed and there is nobody standing by any of them, not even a lonely housewife. The trees are newly planted and thin, sheer new leaves sprout from skinny branches. The only older building is a Mormon church, standing in the middle of a sharp and clean formal landscape like a set out of a black-and-white film. I drift onwards and turn into a street called 300 South Street. Even the streets don't have proper names here – 400 South Street, 500 South Street, 600 South Street, 700 South Street. I walk and walk with only my shadow as a companion; it feels like forever. When I finally near the 'south', I grow desperate – the street names are now 100 E, 200 E, 300 E, 400 E... Then I spot a city map and hope to find some explanation, but it shows that the streets here go up to 2200 E Street. At that point, I feel that life is even more meaningless than yesterday when Li Kai made his announcement.

A lonesome bench in a concrete park seems to be waiting for me. I drag myself towards it. On a nearby bench is a sad black boy eating a hot dog and staring at me. I sit down with my suitcase nestled in between my knees. I open my guidebook and read the first page.

> Salt Lake City is a logically arranged city. All the
> streets labelled West are west of Main Street; all the
> streets labelled East are east of Main Street. Similarly,
> all the streets labelled South are south of South
> Temple Street, and all the streets labelled North are
> north of South Temple Street.

But so what? What's so great about South Temple Street anyway? It then continues.

> Each block in this city is 660 feet or 240 metres
> long, and they are numbered in increments of 100
> Using this street-numbering and distancing system,
> one can easily find one's way around.

Really? I don't think so. I close the guidebook, and look around. There is not a living soul on the streets; even the black boy who was eating his hot dog has vanished. The only thing I can see are hotels, one after the other, lined up on 300 South Street – Hilton Hotel, Marriott Hotel, City Inn, etc., each one with marble walls and American flags blowing in the wind, welcoming invisible guests. Occasionally a doorman shows up in front of a hotel entrance, bored, waiting for nothingness. I take a breath; I feel like I too am turning to marble in front of these buildings. I feel dreadful; I walk on, pulling my heavy suitcase along the asphalt road. The only living, moving things in this world are my two feet and the wheels of the suitcase screeching grittily.

I raise my head at the sound of unidentified noise coming from some unidentified place. The American flag is still blowing on top of the massive building. I don't have an American passport. I don't belong here.

I get on the first bus I see – I don't care where it is going. After drifting along the highway for an hour, I arrive at a tourist resort in Utah. This is the mountain of Wasatch – an Indian name, so the driver announces. I get off the bus with a group of fat white tourists, and hear them say that many rich people have their holiday houses here. Leaving my luggage on the bus, I walk towards the hill and get on a cable chair which will carry me up a 6,000-foot high mountain. Fifteen minutes later, I find myself sitting in the middle of the sky, the purring cable chair slowly pulling me towards the summit. The valley underneath my feet is green and mysterious, the little villas and holiday houses, with their large private swimming pools, elegantly poised on the mountainside – a perfect vantage point to make the most of the surrounding view. People must be really rich here, and I think again that there is absolutely no similarity between this state and my province of Guang Xi. As I fly higher and higher in the cable chair I grow nervous, I can't bear to look down. The wind lifts my trousers, tearing my hair and my flimsy shirt in all directions. Then, right on the top of a deep valley, the cable's regular humming stops, the chair freezes in mid-air, and so do my nerves and blood. The wind is blowing the whole valley below my body. I feel like weeping aloud.

Then, as I lift my head, sitting alone in the opposite cable chair facing the valley, I see a man, his chair rocking back and forth in the silent wind. He stops just ten metres away from me. Holding the metal bar in front of his chest, he looks like some statue hanging in the sky. And then, when our eyes meet, only then, I realise that he looks exactly like a film actor I have seen so many times. We both stare at each other, and I'm no longer scared to die alone in the sky. My mind suddenly starts to move fast. I see a sequence of moving pictures with Robert Redford in it – *The Horse Whisperer*, in which Tom the cowboy talks into a horse's ears and then the mother of the injured girl falls in love with him. Or, the gangster partner of Paul Newman in *The Sting*. Or, the British hunter who made Meryl Streep fall in love with him in *Out Of Africa*...

A shake from the cable; we start moving again, and the Hollywood films disappear. As our hanging chairs cross in silence, I lock my eyes on the man opposite. I cannot believe my eyes, it is Robert Redford himself! Only a bit older, his hair a bit greyer. Now I remember – it said in my tour guide that Robert Redford lives in Utah and he has a villa on the mountain. It must be him! While I'm staring at the figure in the sky, Robert Redford and I pass each other, in silence. Only the sound of the wind. The sound of the wind without Indians and Mormons.

★

Standing on top of the mountain, I look down at the world below like a saint studying the tiny living beings on earth. It's cold and deadly silent here; I feel lonely. The loneliness hits me, and eats me slowly. This moment is worse than any second and any minute in my life. I think of Robert Redford, then I think of Li Kai in the aeroplane to China. I think of people eating, sleeping, moving or arguing in this world. I feel an urge to run away from here. I raise my feet and I step onto the long and silent grass. I walk towards the world underneath me.

FLOWER OF SOLITUDE

1. Houyi

At that time, the universe had two different worlds – the Earth, where the Mortals lived, and the Heaven where the Immortals reigned. At that time, the mountain was scarlet red and the sea flowed with the colour of blood. At that time, the animals crowded the land so much so that the humans had to fight for their space.

At that time, the greatest quality a man could have was to be the best archer. And at that time in those distant ancient days, on the red earth, there was a great archer named Houyi.

With a large bow on his shoulder, Houyi walks rapidly on the wild grass like a leopard streaking through the forest. He heads towards the village of White Elephant to help the locals shoot the wolves – the carnivorous wolves who have recently stolen several babies and left a bloody trail on the path to the woods. No animal, wolf, bull or lion can outrun Houyi's arrows. Houyi is indeed the master of all archers within the kingdom.

The sun burns above the pine trees, and beneath them Houyi sweats like a young bull. He washes his face in a stream at the foot of the hills, drinking in the clear and sweet water from the mountain. He bites into the sour fruit from a wild pear tree, spitting the hard skin onto the grass. He is a man with rough temper; his young beard is thick and strong, always flying in the wind. And with his great silver bow against the arrows on his back, even tigers fear him and slink from his path.

One autumn afternoon, when the heat subsides, Houyi manages to shoot three wolves in the forest. The first two are killed instantly, the third one is wounded and saved for the autumn sacrifice. The villagers celebrate their hero. Some thank Houyi with gifts of corn and fish, others offer smoked pork. Loaded with food, carrying his magnificent bow, Houyi leaves the village.

Houyi's young wife, Chang'e, is alone at home. Gathering silk from cocoons, she prepares to weave winter clothes for Houyi. Wilted and desolate, she feels lonely after marrying her husband, yet she is only fifteen years old. Houyi is just three years older than her, but he is never at home, he is a wild man who loves to make war with nature. And now Chang'e has been chased and won by him, there is nothing left to be done.

With love absent from his mind, he spends his days hunting the forest animals. His young wife has no one with whom to share each passing day except an old magnolia tree standing outside her bedroom window. Chang'e often contemplates its thick leaves and white flowers. She feels like a silent and faint petal of a magnolia flower, waiting for the seasons to bring her back to the earth, yet she herself has no weight and no power.

Every night, Houyi the archer falls asleep straight after supper. His breath is solid and deep, yet as she lies beside her husband Chang'e feels her motionless life wending its way towards a slow death. She sees the shape of her own death as beside Houyi's earthy body. The shape of death, like an ink blot, expands and seeps into the clear area, and eventually swallows the whole visible space, leaving only blackness.

2. Chang'e

Before marrying Houyi, Chang'e was a flower picker in the king's palace. The king was very old. His kingdom was in the southern part of Han China, a land whose tribes ceaselessly fought each other. When Chang'e turned twelve years old she became a servant for one of the king's wives, and had to look after a garden where three jasmine trees grew. Her job was to pick the white flowers of the jasmine trees before they bloomed, then soak them with iced sugar in a jade jar. After a few days the king's wife would drink the sugared jasmine tea to cure her weak lungs.

Each jasmine flower in that garden grew only one single

petal, a white petal in the shape of a heart. They were very fragile. As soon as the slightest wind blew, the petals would fall from the trees like snow. Chang'e had to pick the flowers before the wind came. Day after day Chang'e's young heart endured the monotony of her caged life.

One day, as Chang'e left the king's palace to go to the market to buy sugar, she bumped into a strong handsome man with a great silver bow. Chang'e and Houyi fell in love at first sight. Before long she left the king's jasmine garden, and became the wife of the great archer. Being a young wife, Chang'e raises silkworms under the mulberry trees, cooks rice and soup on top of a pile of chopped tree trunks, washes clothes in a nearby river. She knows the archer loves her, but her lonely heart drifts inside her empty chest. She feels love for him, but somehow it fades away, little by little, each night while Houyi sleeps. She doesn't know what she lives for any more. She feels again that she is back in the old king's jasmine garden, under the same burning sun, raising her tired arms, picking each delicate flower, for no purpose from one day to the next.

3. Wu Gang

At that time, above the great Chinese sky, there was a Heaven, where all the Immortals live. The Emperor of Heaven had the power to decide who could live there, and who could not.

Yet for Wu Gang, the impulsive Emperor of Heaven made a different decision. Wu Gang's fate was to abide forever in the limbo between the Immortal and Mortal worlds. He became the gatekeeper of the South Heaven Gate – the only passage from Earth to Heaven.

Motionless and empty, Wu Gang leans against the South Heaven Gate, reminiscing over moments of his past life on Earth. He was once a woodcutter in a bamboo forest. Each morning he woke to the sound of birds, washed himself in a blue lake, and then spent his days chopping down trees for his tribe. He was happy with his life. Somehow the Emperor of Heaven judged Wu Gang to be no ordinary man, but rather the most trustful person on earth. So the Greatest Mind chose Wu Gang to guard the heavenly gate, and ever since then Wu Gang has been living in this void. He misses his homeland and using his solid axe on solid bamboo, better than this heavenly axe he is forced to wield. He misses the smell of the earth after thunderstorms and the sound of the river flowing behind his bamboo shed. Now he is in limbo, an interim space, and a lifeless zone where the earth ends and the unreachable Heaven begins. He is in a world where there is no sound, no colour and no weight. Only Wu Gang's axe has a firm shape. He can see his body but can't feel his own weight. The people chosen by the Emperor of Heaven to become Immortals merely pass through Wu Gang's gate. No one has ever stayed with him to talk of Earth, and besides, there is no concrete space by that gate where one could rest. Wu Gang lives in a flow of air, from which he can only contemplate the Earth through the ethereal clouds. He is the loneliest being in the universe.

★

One day, through deep layers of clouds, Wu Gang's eyes catch sight of the beautiful Chang'e while she is standing under a jasmine tree in the king's garden, the jasmine blossoms raining down like snow in the wind. Chang'e leans by the tree, gazing at those petals falling all around her. Rays of light caress her hair and neck. The gatekeeper is stunned by her delicate beauty. He starts to mutter to himself, wishing he could become her companion, to comfort and embrace her through life. But how? He is no longer a man of flesh, he is only half-man half-spirit, without weight or gravity.

Every passing day Wu Gang watches the jasmine garden from the high and distant South Heaven Gate. The lonely man rests against the gate with his humble axe, his half-life seeming a little less empty, until one day Chang'e disappears from the jasmine garden. He looks for her with his half-human eyes, but his sight has lost its power in the overly crowded human world. He cannot see even a trace of her among the mist, rain and smoke, among the shoulders in the market, the feet on the bridges, the hats in the fields. Heavy-hearted, he thinks that in her earthly life, she must have become someone's wife, now living under a roof, cooking for a family. Thinking of such a life, his heart turns cold as his vision of the earth becomes blurred. From solitude his heart grows as hard as a granite stone, he can no longer feel the tender emotion that once possessed him. The day goes on, the night slips away. Wu Gang senses something sorrowful in the world beneath him, yet this sorrow is lost in the thin air and he no longer recognises human emotion.

4. The Hottest Day

Then one day the earth becomes unbearably hot. It's so hot that the hills of the Gobi Desert burn like a volcano. The bamboo forests in the southern hemisphere are dry and dead from lack of rain, the pinewoods in the north are burnt into black ashes. Even the old king breathes his last on that day. When the people learn that the old king has died, the whole kingdom cries out in desperation.

But Houyi the archer raises his dark eyes towards the sky. His eyes are as sharp as the arrow on his bow. Through the floating clouds and formless wind, he sees seven suns hanging in the sky. In ancient time of legend, the Heaven Bird was transformed into a blazing sun, created to shine upon the earthly world. At that time, there were seven Heaven Birds living in the sky and they were the playthings of the greatest Heaven Emperor. At that time, each sun bird was only allowed to come out from the Heavenly Empire once every seven days. But on this hottest day, the suns disobey their master and appear in the sky together, unaware of the enormous damage they are doing to the earth. The great archer Houyi cannot restrain his anger any longer, furiously he draws six silver arrows out of his leopardskin sack. Whizz, whizz, whizz...one after another, he shoots down six suns, each in one strike!

The hills of the Gobi Desert suddenly stop burning, the bamboo forests in the south are immediately awash with rain and the pinewood fire gradually abates. Men and women in the fields recover from their terror; tigers and lions emerge from their deep caves and roam again on the plains.

The following day, the people unanimously agree to elect the great archer Houyi the new king of their country. With Chang'e he moves into the old king's palace. And now Chang'e is back in her one-petal jasmine-tree garden where now all trees belong to her and all the servants have become her servants. She doesn't have to make jasmine sugar tea for another woman any more. Instead King Houyi orders magicians and herbalists from throughout the land to hunt down rare herbs with which to make the elixir of longevity. For many centuries experts have tried to find the secret recipe for this potion, but with no success. Nevertheless, each new king orders his people to continue to make this magic powder. The great archer wants to be immortal, as all previous kings of the land.

But the Heaven Emperor is in rage. Not only has this new king killed six of his pet birds but he also has the audacity to want to be immortal! How dare he! The Heaven Emperor considers how best to punish Houyi. In Heaven, there are four levels of punishment. The lightest one is Sorrow, then comes Fear. The third level is the absolute Loneliness. And the most cruel punishment of all is absolute Despair. With an impulsive temper and a thoughtless mind, the Heaven Emperor decides that the new King Houyi deserves the highest punishment. So Houyi becomes the most despairing man on Earth. He sees no future in life, he distrusts everyone in the kingdom, he has no belief in love, and he thinks of death in every quiet moment.

Every night, lying beside Houyi, Chang'e inhales the new

king's despairing breath and, as before, she perceives in each of her husband's sighs their flesh rotten in an airless tomb, bones dissolving in the vegetable roots. The death ink is seeping into the night, darkening their life with total obscurity. She is fearful − fearful of a future doomed by fate. One night, Chang'e gets up, steals the key from Houyi's robe and enters the castle where the specialists make the elixir of longevity. She finds a huge jade jar and, tentatively lifting the lid, she smells bitter roots. She takes the glowing liquid back to her quarters. Then the next night she leaves her bed and does the same again, collecting as much as she can. After three hundred and sixty-six days and nights, her task is complete. She holds in her hand the essence of immortality. She stands under the one-petal jasmine tree and drains all the precious medicine while Houyi lies in a depressed sleep. Before the rooster breaks the dawn, she finds herself starting to float − she is flying, flying, and flying. She passes the South Heaven Gate, where Wu Gang is still asleep, and enters into the realm of the shining moon.

5. Moon

The Emperor of Heaven is angry again. He wants to punish Wu Gang for not paying attention to his job, and letting a human being enter the world of the Immortals. So the Great Impulsive Mind decides to expel Wu Gang from his job and impose upon him the greatest Sorrow. He sends Wu Gang to the moon to chop a cinnamon tree. This is how the Sorrow is inflicted upon him: as soon as Wu Gang stops chopping the tree, it grows back again even stronger and thicker. His punishment never ends.

In the moon, all Wu Gang wants is to be mortal again, to return to the Earth and be a man. But when he raises his axe on the lonely cinnamon tree in the space of silver, he discovers another human being – Chang'e, the most beautiful girl, the one he saw in the jasmine-tree garden all those years ago. The sight of Chang'e reanimates his heart with a vague emotion, as her eyes are the loneliest he has ever encountered. The sight of her face clutches at his heart, but it is too withered from the long absence of love. He strains to remember how he felt towards people when he was on the Earth. He tries to recognise Chang'e, her human emotion – her fragile flesh which envelops her heart. During shadowless days and nights on the moon Wu Gang tries to recover the feeling of his heart, while ceaselessly chopping down the stubborn tree. Perhaps Wu Gang is no longer the most sorrowful man in the universe. He is with Chang'e, who reflects the only recognisable human feeling still inside him. But while the cinnamon leaves keep falling on Chang'e's hair, she transforms into a being of absolute solitude. Her soul dwells nowhere. In her formlessness, she understands that a chasm of separation exists between her and the earth, and that she must accept this absolute solitude, for death is no longer her destiny.

As the image of the Earth subsides in Wu Gang's mind, all he can do is to chop the cinnamon tree, day after day. He sweats, sweats, and sweats from exhaustion. And on Earth it rains, drenching the warm soil from time to time, rain that is the sweat of a man's labour. King Houyi stands under his jasmine tree and looks up into the dark sky above; he sees two human shadows on the moon with his great archer's eyes. He senses that these rains on the Earth are born from that land of silver.

Each moonlit night, in the absence of Chang'e, the despairing King Houyi steps silently on the withered, one-petalled flowers deeply buried in his soil. He contemplates the moon, yearning for his long-lost companion, in the abyss of absolute solitude.

ACKNOWLEDGEMENTS

As well as the muffled but intense whisperings I heard on
the road, these beautiful people helped to shape this book:
Rebecca Morris, Pamela Casey, Philippe Ciompi, Juliet
Brooke, Clara Farmer, Rebecca Carter, Claire Paterson, Steve
Barker, Rao Hui, Simon Chambers, Rebecca Folland, Tina
Bennett, Klaus Maeck, Anne Rademacher, Susanne Klumpp,
Cindy Carter and Enda Hugh.

Xiaolu Guo, 2009
Germany – England